M. C. Beaton is [illegible]
Agatha Raisin and [illegible]
as a quartet of Edward[illegible]
ing heroine Lady Rose Su[illegible]
romance series and a stand-alone murd[illegible]
The Skeleton in the Closet – all published by Constable & Robinson. She left a full-time career in journalism to turn to writing, and now divides her time between the Cotswolds and Paris. For more details, visit www.agatharaisin.com, or follow M. C. Beaton on Twitter:@mc_beaton.

Regency romance series by M. C. Beaton

Regency Scandal
His Lordship's Pleasure • Her Grace's Passion • The Scandalous Lady Wright

The School for Manners
Refining Felicity • Perfecting Fiona • Enlightening Delilah
Finessing Clarissa • Animating Maria • Marrying Harriet

The Poor Relation
Lady Fortescue Steps Out • Miss Tonks Turns to Crime
Mrs Budley Falls from Grace • Sir Philip's Folly
Colonel Sandhurst to the Rescue • Back in Society

A House for the Season
The Miser of Mayfair • Plain Jane • The Wicked Godmother
Rake's Progress • The Adventuress • Rainbird's Revenge

The Six Sisters
Minerva • The Taming of Annabelle • Deirdre and Desire
Daphne • Diana the Huntress • Frederica in Fashion

The Travelling Matchmaker
Emily Goes to Exeter • Belinda Goes to Bath • Penelope Goes to Portsmouth
Beatrice Goes to Brighton • Deborah Goes to Dover • Yvonne Goes to York

Also available

Edwardian Murder Mysteries
Snobbery with Violence • Hasty Death • Sick of Shadows
Our Lady of Pain

The Scandalous Lady Wright

M. C. Beaton

Constable • London

CONSTABLE

This paperback edition published in Great Britain in 2014

All characters and events in this publication, other than those clearly in the public domain, are fictitious and any resemblance to real persons, living or dead, is purely coincidental.

A CIP catalogue record for this book
is available from the British Library.

ISBN: 978-1-4721-1211-8 (paperback)
ISBN: 978-1-4721-0147-1 (ebook)

Typeset by TW Typesetting, Plymouth, Devon.
Printed and bound in Great Britain by
CPI Group (UK) Ltd, Croydon, CR0 4YY.

Constable
is an imprint of
Constable & Robinson Ltd
100 Victoria Embankment
London EC4Y 0DY

An Hachette UK Company
www.hachette.co.uk

www.constablerobinson.com

1 3 5 7 9 10 8 6 4 2

Contents

ONE

'So you are to leave us again, Lady Wright?'

Miss Appleby, a thin, eager young lady, all sharp corners – sharp elbows, sharp nose and sharp eyes – stared enviously at Emma, Lady Wright. There was much to envy, thought Miss Appleby. Not only was Lady Wright very beautiful, but she was married to Sir Benjamin Wright, Member of Parliament and distinguished leader of the small society of the village of Upper Tipton in Sussex.

'Yes,' said Emma quietly, 'Sir Benjamin does not like to stay away from the House too long,' by which she meant the House of Commons. Silently Emma sent up a prayer that Miss Appleby and the rest of the guests would go so that she could finish her preparations for the journey on the morrow. The people who were gathered in the Wrights' drawing room consisted of the upper class of the village.

Apart from Miss Appleby, there was the squire, Sir Harry Henley, and his wife and two sons, Lady Herriet, a grim dowager, the rector, Dr Barnstable, his wife and daughter, and old Colonel Anderson, long retired from the wars but still fighting them in extensive monologues, and Emma's parents, Mr and Mrs Anstey, looking nervous and honoured at being included in such exalted company.

The guests all had one thing in common: they were proud of Sir Benjamin, and eagerly cut out reports of his speeches from the newspapers and circulated them around the less distinguished members of the village. He was a tall, corpulent man with a thick head of white hair, a long body and short little legs. He looked impressive sitting down. He had paleblue eyes criss-crossed with a network of red veins, for Sir Benjamin was fond of the bottle.

Emma had been married to him for three years. She had never been asked whether she wanted to marry Sir Benjamin or not. He had seen her at a local charity ball, had approached her parents, and settled the matter with them.

At first Emma had quietly accepted the idea of marriage to him. He was very rich indeed. She had seven sisters and three brothers. Her father was a gentleman and so did not work, living on a small yearly income from a family trust. Although five of her sisters and two brothers were now married, they had not married well, and so it was Emma, because of her strange and rare beauty, who had been picked to restore the family fortunes. Whatever Sir

Benjamin had paid for her by way of the marriage settlements, Emma did not know, but often reflected her father must have driven a hard bargain, for the Ansteys now boasted a smart new carriage and had moved to a larger house on the outskirts of the village.

Emma hardly saw her family. Sir Benjamin had let it be known that he had married beneath him and would be pleased if the connection were cut. The invitation to her parents was a rare mark of condescension. Emma remembered well trying to talk to her mother about the hell that was her marriage, but her mother had looked shocked and would not listen.

And so Emma, humiliated in the bedroom and tyrannized outside of it, had retreated into herself, hiding in the rooms of her mind, where her husband could not reach her.

She felt she might have died of sheer loneliness of spirit had not a miracle happened during the last London Season.

She rose and walked over to the pianoforte and sat down and began to play so that she could remember that miracle in peace. Behind her, the guests drank and gossiped as her fingers moved across the keys.

Last year the Season had been nearly over when her husband had insisted she make a call on an elderly dowager, Mrs Trumpington, whose husband had been a prominent member of the Whig party during his lifetime. He had intended to go with her, but had drunk so deeply the night before that he complained of being poisoned and said he would spend the day in bed.

And so Emma had gone alone. There were two other ladies there visiting Mrs Trumpington, both, like Emma, in their early twenties. They were Annabelle, Mrs Carruthers, married to a gamester; and Matilda, Duchess of Hadshire. Mrs Trumpington proved to be a malicious and amusing old quiz and entertained her guests with all the latest scandal before suddenly and quietly falling asleep.

The three ladies had talked politely at first about the things they were supposed to talk about, social chitchat, recipes, plays and operas, but all of them being drawn together by the fact that all were as yet childless.

And then Emma had said suddenly, after they had been discussing a production of *Romeo and Juliet*, 'I wonder what would have happened had Romeo been able to marry his Juliet? Perhaps after a year or two passed, he would be nagging her about this and that, and she would have grown fat on pasta and misery.'

'Or he would have drunk and gambled so that life became a constant fear of ruins and duns,' said Annabelle.

'Or his great love might prove to be nothing more than a sophisticated fantasy,' said Matilda. They talked for a little, and then it dawned on Emma that they were in fact all talking about their husbands. It was so delicious to be able to unburden oneself to sympathetic ears that each lady began to castigate Romeo and that famous lover began to take on the character of first Emma's husband, then Annabelle's, and then Matilda's. They became fast friends. Sir Benjamin was flattered that one of his wife's new friends was a duchess and did everything he could to encourage the friendship.

And soon I shall see them again, thought Emma as her fingers rippled over the keys. It had been a grim winter. The deeper Sir Benjamin sank into the bottle, the more malicious and autocratic he became. He never staggered or slurred his speech; he merely became vindictive. He had decided that his pretty wife's inability to breed was caused by her lack of enthusiasm in the bedroom, and his demands on her body became more innovative and, to Emma, more humiliating. Although he stayed some time in London to attend the parliamentary debates in the House of Commons, such stays were of miserably short duration, or so it seemed to Emma. Each evening he was at home she would pray with increasing fervour that he would pass out as soon as his head hit the pillow, and for the past blessed month that had been the case.

If only he would drink himself to death! Emma shuddered at the wicked thought, but it took hold of her mind. She could almost see the funeral, the churchyard, the mourners. She could hear the voice of the rector raised in the funeral service; she imagined she could feel the springy turf of the graveyard under her feet as she walked away from the graveside a free woman.

Her husband put a hand on her shoulder and she started in alarm and brought her fingers down on the keys in a noisy discord. The harsh sound echoed round the drawing room.

'Our guests are going, my love,' said Sir Benjamin.

Emma rose gracefully, lowering her eyes in case he could read her thoughts, and went to say good-bye. She kissed her mother's cold, powdered cheek. Her father gave her a perfunctory nod, his eyes already swivelling in the direction of Sir Benjamin in hope of some more marks of favour about which he could tell his cronies.

As soon as the last guest had gone, Emma slipped quietly away to her room to check that everything necessary had been packed. Her maid undressed her and prepared her for bed and then withdrew. Emma lay for a long time awake, dreading to see the door open and her husband standing on the threshold. At last she heard him mounting the stairs with a slow, dragging step and held her breath. His hand fumbled at the knob of her door, and then he slowly went along to his own room. Still Emma lay awake until at last the slow rumbling sound of snoring echoed along the corridor.

Safe for one more blessed night!

Tomorrow they would travel to London and she would see her friends again.

Sir Benjamin was in a foul mood as they set out for London. His head throbbed and ached and the light hurt his eyes. He felt obscurely that his miserable condition was all his wife's fault and eyed her sourly. Her beauty did nothing to soften his heart. She looked so cool and remote with her shining black curls under a smart bonnet and the calm oval of her face betraying no expression whatsoever and her large and beautiful dark blue eyes as blank as those of a sleepwalker. Her knack of retreating into her own mind and away from him annoyed him and excited him sensually at the same time as it gave the experiences of the marriage bed the extra titillating edge of rape. Sir Benjamin had brutal lusts and had his wife matched those, he would quickly have tired of her.

He knew travelling fatigued her and that the swaying motion of the coach made her feel ill. They were due to arrive in London at five o'clock the following afternoon. He had received an invitation to a ball at the French ambassador's, which he had accepted for both of them, but had meant to send around a letter of apology as soon as they arrived, saying they could not attend. When he had first accepted the invitation, he had forgotten the ball was to take place on the eve of their arrival. But now he thought it might be a good idea to go after all. Emma would hate it. She would be feeling tired and ill.

'We are going to the French ambassador's dinner and ball tomorrow night, Lady Wright,' he said harshly. 'Wear your diamonds.'

A look of dismay crossed her face, but she slightly bowed her head in assent.

Furious that he had been unable to raise any stronger reaction from her, Sir Benjamin jerked her into his arms and began to kiss her with wet, lascivious kisses while one of his strong hands crushed her left breast in a painful grip. Her coldness excited him, and he would have ripped her gown off had it not been for the presence of his wife's lady's maid, Austin, sitting opposite them with her head averted. He finally thrust Emma aside after giving her breast a final tweak. The lady's maid continued to look out of the window. She was every bit as poker-faced as her mistress, he reflected sourly, although, unlike Emma, she had a face like an old boot.

Still, humiliating his wife in front of her maid had put him in a good mood. He drank a great deal when they stopped for refreshment and fell mercifully asleep. Emma, looking at Austin, caught a fleeting look of pity on her lady's maid's face and realized with surprise that her maid was sorry for her. The look was gone as quickly as it had come, but it had most definitely been there, and Emma felt strangely comforted. She had assumed all the servants revered Sir Benjamin as much as did members of the local society of Upper Tipton.

Perhaps it was that little look of compassion that sustained her on the journey and the fact that her husband slept most of the way, for she felt tired but not at all travel sick when the carriage finally rolled to a halt in front of Sir Benjamin's town house in Curzon Street.

Now it was Sir Benjamin who was mentally cursing his own folly in having decided to go to the ball. He was about to send a footman to say they could not attend after all, but Emma had decided that if they went to the ball, then her husband would drink too much and then he would sleep that night without troubling her, and so she put a hand to her forehead and swayed slightly and said, 'I fear I do not think I am well enough to go out this evening, Sir Benjamin.'

'Nonsense!' he said immediately. 'Of course we are going', and Emma looked at him sadly and wearily while inside she was delighted at the success of her little piece of play-acting.

That evening she put on a dark-blue silk gown that matched the colour of her eyes. About her neck she wore the heavy collar of diamonds he had given her, and her thick black hair was coiffed in a simple style without any ornament or feathers. Her clothes were of the finest, Sir Benjamin enjoying showing off his beautiful young wife to London society.

Beautiful though she was, Emma was not a heartbreaker. To the young men who asked her to dance, she appeared too cold and withdrawn to be of any interest.

When they reached the French ambassador's residence, the cream of London society was already arriving. Britain had not long ago ceased fighting the French, but the British still adored everything French, and the long war had done nothing to damp their enthusiasm. All the foreign ambassadors appeared to have turned up along with the British ministers, Lord Castlereagh, Lord Melville, Lord Stewart and Lord Binning.

They sat down to dinner, Emma relieved to find she had been placed next to the American ambassador, Mr Richard Rush, and some distance away from her husband. The Prince Regent was seated next to the French ambassador, the Marquis D'Osmond, and the very presence of his fat and florid regal figure added a lustre to the evening. Everyone affected to despise the prince and yet damned most events at which he was not in attendance as 'deuced flat'.

On the other side of Emma from the American ambassador was an elderly diplomat, Sir Struthers-Wiggins. He was deaf, and so in the ringing tones of those hard of hearing he roared in Emma's ear, 'There's one thing about the Frogs – they know how to cook.'

Emma blushed in embarrassment and turned to the ambassador, but he was discoursing on the problem of Pensacola with his neighbour. Sir Struthers-Wiggins began boring the lady on his other side, and so Emma was left alone. There was, she noticed, a great quantity of wine being served – burgundy, tokay, St Julien, and Sillery champagne. With any luck, her husband would soon be drunk. She had schooled herself to enjoy all brief moments of freedom from his company, and so she ate and drank with enjoyment, planning to call on her friends the next afternoon. The voices about her rose and fell like the waves of the sea. 'General Jackson, commander of the United States, had taken possession of these fortresses not as an act of hostility to Spain, but in necessary prosecution of the war against the Indians, and the defence of our own frontier.' That was the American ambassador, still well launched on the subject of Pensacola. 'I said to my son, I said, "Why go to Paris for your pleasures? A night with Venus means a lifetime with mercury." Haw, haw, haw.' Sir Struthers-Wiggins was disgracing himself thoroughly. Mercury was the treatment for venereal disease.

And then Emma, looking across the table, saw for the first time the man who was to change her life. He was tall, impeccably dressed, with thick fair hair in disordered curls, very blue eyes, and a thin, clever face. He was leaning back in his chair, idly listening to the enthusiastic prattle of the lady beside him, but his blue eyes were fixed on Emma.

She looked quickly down at her plate. She found her hands were trembling and put them under the table and clasped them in her lap. She tentatively looked across at him again. His blue gaze met and held her own for a few moments. She jerked her head away and found to her relief that the American ambassador, Mr Rush, had turned to her.

Emma asked him how he was enjoying London and Mr Rush began to make a statement. He did not converse – he made statements, and so all she had to do was listen and nod from time to time and try so very hard to forget about the blue gaze across the table. 'I must say there is one thing I found offensive,' said Mr Rush. 'At the drop-curtain at Covent Garden are seen the flags of the nations with whom

England has been at war. They are in a shattered state, and represented as being in subjection to England. That of the United States is among them! The symbols are, therefore, not historically true.'

Emma suggested that a letter to the management of Covent Garden, protesting the insult, might be a good idea. Mr Rush approved. She risked another look across the table, but the fair-haired man was now giving his attention to his neighbour. 'Who is that gentleman opposite?' she could not resist asking. 'In the blue evening coat and with fair hair.'

To Emma's dismay, Mr Rush raised his large quizzing glass and peered through it at the fair-haired young man. 'The Comte Saint-Juste,' he said.

'And is he a diplomat?'

'No, he is a friend of the D'Osmonds. A lily of the field. He does nothing.' Mr Rush's voice sounded disapproving.

'But most of society do nothing,' protested Emma. 'Why is this comte so unusual?'

'I mean, he appears to do nothing at all. He has no interest in sport, or literature, or the collection of art. He is a social butterfly. He is to be seen everywhere. His family fled the French Revolution but managed to escape with a great deal of money. He has been educated in England but has the soul of a Frenchman.'

'And is that so very bad? We are no longer at war with France, and even when we were, the English still spoke French in polite society and copied French fashions and engaged French chefs.'

'It is impossible to talk to that young man about any of the affairs of state,' said Mr Rush, ignoring her question. 'He has no interest in anything other than his clothes and his horses.'

He smiled at Emma, thinking how pleasant it was to have such a beautiful companion at the dinner table. Lady Wright, married as she was to such a prominent member of the British Parliament, must surely despise these useless society fribbles such as the Comte Saint-Juste.

The lady on the other side of Mr Rush caught his attention again and he reluctantly turned away from Emma.

But his disparaging remarks only had the effect of making the comte more interesting in Emma's eyes. Her husband's friends discussed politics, hunting or club gossip. It would be fascinating to talk to a man who was interested in nothing in particular.

The lengthy dinner was at last over and the guests removed to the ballroom, where the orchestra was already playing. Emma noticed two footmen helping her husband from the room. He appeared to be very drunk. Her eyes scanned the other guests, hoping that her friends, Matilda and Annabelle, might have arrived late, but there was no sign of them. Perhaps something had happened and they had decided not to come to London for the Season. But that was so bleak a thought that she thrust it away.

She sat down on a little gilt chair in a corner of the ballroom, unfurled her fan, and fanned herself slowly and languidly, suddenly weary after the long journey.

There was an arrangement of hothouse plants in tubs between her and the ballroom floor. Her eyelids began to droop. With any luck she could sit quietly until it was time to go home. She knew her husband would sleep off the worst of his drunkenness in some anteroom and then would come and look for her. She remembered with a shudder his wrath the first time in their marriage when this had happened and she had assumed he had left and so had gone home. He had burst into her bedroom and slapped her across the face for having *dared* to leave without him.

Dancers were making up sets for the quadrille. The ballroom was very hot. Suddenly, as in a dream, she heard a light, pleasant voice saying, 'No, I beg you, *ma chère marquise*, it is better we leave the sleeping beauty alone!'

She slowly raised her heavy lids and then started in confusion. The Comte Saint-Juste with the Marquise D'Osmond at his elbow was smiling down at her.

Emma rose, blushing, and dropped a low curtsy. 'Pray, forgive me, Madame la Marquise,' she said. 'I am fatigued having arrived only this day from the country.'

'Do not distress yourself,' said the little marquise. 'Lady Wright, may I present the Comte Saint-Juste. My dear comte . . . the Lady Wright.'

He gave a magnificent bow, elegantly waving a lace-edged handkerchief with many flourishes.

'My husband . . . ?' said Emma, looking nervously about her. 'He must be looking for me.'

'Sir Benjamin is asleep in the library,' replied the marquise. 'He sleeps well. I shall rouse him in a little while. Ah, you must excuse me. I must attend to my other guests.'

She trotted off, leaving Emma alone with the comte.

He pulled a chair forward. 'You permit? It would be pleasant to sit quietly for a moment.'

Emma curtsied again and sat down, fanning herself nervously.

The comte studied her curiously. She had high cheekbones that gave her face an almost Slavic look. Her mouth was beautifully shaped and a deep pink against the whiteness of her skin. Her eyes were guarded and wary.

Emma looked back at him. He did not have that wooden look so fashionable among the members of the ton. He had a high-nosed, clever, mobile face. His eyes were very blue and fringed with thick black lashes. He was tall with a slim, athletic figure and very good legs. He could surely not lead such an indolent life as that described by Mr Rush. He did not bear any marks of dissipation in his face or figure.

'And what is the result of your inspection?' he mocked.

Emma realized she had been staring at him and raised her fan to her face. His voice was light and pleasant but with a definite French accent.

‘I hear you were educated in England, Monsieur le Comte,’ she said, ‘and yet you have a French accent.’

‘My poor parents were sure that at any moment order would be restored in France and their lands returned to them. My education was by French tutors. I did not speak English until I went to university. And such English! *Ma foi!* Imagine the English of a young man who had learned that language from grooms in the stables. I cursed like a trooper.’

‘And do you hope to return to France at some time?’

He shrugged. ‘I go back from time to time. It is so depressing. There is barely a whole man in France – arms missing, legs missing, all the horrors of war. But such are not things for your pretty ears to hear. I would rather tell you that you are possessed of a rare beauty.’

‘And I would rather you did not,’ replied Emma tartly. ‘I am married.’

‘And still asleep.’

‘I was fatigued after today’s journey. I am a bad traveller.’

‘I did not mean that. I meant that no man has awakened you yet.’

Emma regarded him steadily. ‘You insult me and my husband. Please leave me.’

‘I apologize from the bottom of my heart. You have the right of it. We shall talk of social things. Shall I tell you the latest on-dit? Mrs Bambury, that lady of impeccable breeding and icy manners, eloped some time back with her footman. La! The disgrace and the prophecies of doom. It appeared her husband beat her and made her life hell, but everyone sympathized with *him.* Is that not the English way? Mrs Bambury, the *fallen* Mrs Bambury, would end up dying of poverty in some ditch, said everyone. She fled with her footman to America. With her jewels the young footman bought land in Virginia and prospered. Last seen, the fallen Mrs Bambury is a deliriously happy and wealthy lady. I do not think London society will ever forgive her. I do, of course, for I made a great deal of money out of her.'

'How so?' asked Emma, trying not to laugh, for there was something comical about the rapidly changing expressions on his face.

'When they were all predicting the ruination of Mrs Bambury, I thought about that strong lady and her young and powerful footman and *I* bet a great number of gentlemen that the odd liaison would prosper. I am proved to be right. I collect my bets. You remind me of Mrs Bambury.'

'You find my manners icy?'

'On the contrary, Lady Wright, you are neither icy nor haughty, but, like Mrs Bambury, I feel you have a great strength of character and great courage.'

'Believe me, Monsieur le Comte, I am hardly likely to form a tendre for one of my footmen. I find you conversation shocking.'

'You have the right of it,' he said, getting to his feet. Emma felt a pang of disappointment. He was going to leave her. So many men found her dull.

But how could she sparkle and be amusing when the thought of her violent and brutish husband lay always across her mind like a dark thunder-cloud?

'So we shall dance,' he said, holding out his hand.

There was a gaiety, an irresponsibility about him that was very infectious. Emma suddenly smiled and the comte caught his breath. That smile brought her to life. Her large eyes sparkled and her stolen youth came back to her.

The dance was a waltz. Emma felt his hand at her waist and looked up into those laughing, mocking blue eyes and forgot about Sir Benjamin and lived only for that dance. He smelled of clean linen and soap. He danced beautifully. The ballroom swam around them, candles and flowers and jewels melting into a blur. The Marquise D'Osmond stopped dancing and drew her partner aside so that they could watch the comte and Emma. Others followed suit.

Sir Benjamin awoke in the library and lay in an armchair, staring at the ceiling and wondering for a moment where he was. Then memory came flooding back. His head ached and his mouth felt dry. He lurched to his feet. Better get his wife and go home.

He went into the ballroom. Everyone was grouped around the dance floor, watching some couple dancing. His bleary eyes focused on the couple, and he let out a gasp of pure rage.

There was his Emma, radiant and beautiful and alive, making an exhibition of herself in the arms of some mountebank. He wanted to rush onto the floor and drag her away but was mindful, even in his rage, of his position as a member of His Majesty's government. The Prince Regent appeared to have left, but Sir Benjamin knew he could not make a scene in front of the world's ambassadors.

At last, after what seemed like an age, that dreadful, haunting waltz music died away. The audience applauded. He made his way to Emma's side and took her arm above the elbow in a cruel grip.

'Time we left, m'dear,' he said in a voice thick with suppressed rage.

And all the lights went out, thought the comte, watching the extinguished look on Emma's face, watching how her whole body, so pliant in the waltz, stiffened. He bowed as Sir Benjamin, looking neither to the right nor the left, marched his wife from the floor like a jailor, convinced he was acting discreetly, and yet creating almost as much attention as if he had publicly slapped her.

In the carriage on the way home, the floodgates of Sir Benjamin's wrath burst. He called Emma a slut. He said she would be locked in her room that night and whipped before all the servants in the hall in the morning. And worse than any of this to Emma, he told her her friends Annabelle and Matilda were a bad influence and he forbade her to see them again.

In vain did Emma cry out in their defence, saying they had only just arrived in London and she had, therefore, had no opportunity of seeing her friends. He struck her across the mouth to silence her, and as she raised a handkerchief to staunch the blood from her cut and bruised lips, he said he would call on that man-milliner with whom she had been dancing in the morning and command that fribble to keep away from his wife. He demanded to know his name, but Emma said she had not caught his name when the Marquise D'Osmond had introduced them. Sir Benjamin was forced to believe the lie, for he did not dream for a moment that his wife would have enough courage to do other than tell him the truth.

When they reached the house, once more holding Emma tightly by the arm Sir Benjamin summoned all the servants. In ringing tones he told Tamworthy, the butler, that Lady Wright was to be locked in her bedchamber and publicly whipped in the morning. He himself was going to his study and was not to be disturbed. He wanted all the servants in their quarters for the rest of the night.

Emma pulled away from him. 'You monster!' she shouted. 'I wish you were dead! I could kill you!'

'By the time I have finished with you, madam,' he grated, 'you will be praying for your own death.' He signalled to Austin, the lady's maid. 'Take your mistress upstairs,' he commanded. 'Prepare her for bed, lock the door, and give the key to Tamworthy.'

Head held high, Emma walked up the stairs with her maid hurrying after her. She sat like stone while the silent maid brushed her hair and then helped her to undress and prepared her for bed.

'That will be all, Austin,' said Emma. 'You may leave me.'

'My lady,' said Austin, keeping her eyes lowered, 'if you would allow me to fetch some salve for your mouth from the stillroom.'

'No, Austin,' said Emma wearily. 'It does not matter. Nothing matters now.'

Austin curtsied and went out and shut the door. A moment later Emma heard the key turn in the lock.

She sat up against the pillows, her eyes hard and dry. No, this time she would not cry. She was past tears. She was married to a monster, and her own parents would not step in to save her.

She knew Sir Benjamin would carry out his threat in the morning. He was an insanely jealous man. He was not only jealous of her affections, but jealous of every other Member of Parliament who was capable of commanding more attention than himself – and there were many. There must be some way out. Any sort of life was better than the one into which she was locked and fettered by the bonds of matrimony.

She would defy him. When he left for the House, she would escape and go to see Matilda and Annabelle and beg their help. They must find some way to get her out of the country.

She thought of the comte's story of Mrs Bambury. There was a woman who had managed to escape the laws of society. She wished with all her heart and soul that her husband would die.

She knew he kept a loaded pistol in the drawer of the desk in his study. He was always complaining about Irish terrorists or the number of burglars in London. The house was locked and bolted and shuttered at night like a prison. Wires and clusters of alarm bells were placed on the downstairs windows, where any forced entry would set them jangling through the night. Emma thought longingly that if she could escape from her room, she might be able to go down to the study, take out that pistol, and shoot her husband through the heart. It was only a fantasy. But a very vivid one.

So vivid was it that when the sound of a pistol shot rang through the house, she turned pale, thinking for one awful moment that she had run mad and turned fantasy into reality. She got out of bed and tried the door of her bedroom, but it was firmly locked. She leaned her head against the panels of the door and listened hard. But there was no commotion, no sound of running feet.

And then she gave a little sigh. Of course, it had happened before. Insanely drunk on two occasions, Sir Benjamin had imagined burglars in the house and had fired his pistol. He must have started drinking again in his study.

Emma climbed back into bed. Despite her distress and fear, her eyes began to close and soon she was fast asleep.

TWO

Emma was awakened the following morning by a piercing scream echoing through the house. She lay still for a moment and then leapt from the bed and ran to the door and hammered on it. Light footsteps came running up the stairs and along the corridor. She heard the key click in the lock and then the door opened.

Austin stood there, her eyes dilated with fright. 'It's Sir Benjamin, my lady,' she cried. 'He's dead!'

Guilt and shock would soon follow, but all in that moment Emma felt weak with relief. So he had finally drunk himself to death.

'Where is he, Austin?' she asked. 'Are you sure? Have you sent for the physician?'

'Oh, he's dead as dead. Tamworthy's sent for the magistrate and the constable.'

'Does one need a parish constable to record a natural death?'

'He was shot. Shot through the heart.'

Emma raised her hands to her face. 'It's not possible,' she whispered.

'My lady,' said Austin, 'pray sit down. I had no right to burst out with the news like that. Oh, my poor lady.'

'No, no, Austin, you must help me dress. I must do what I can. I heard a pistol shot during the night, but I assumed Sir Benjamin had imagined there to be burglars in the house again.'

'That's what Tamworthy said, my lady.' Austin searched the wardrobe and brought out a sombre black gown, which Emma had worn six months before to attend the funeral of one of Sir Benjamin's relatives. 'He heard the shot, but you know Sir Benjamin said he wasn't to be disturbed . . . but Tamworthy became worried when Mary took up the master's tea this morning and found his bed not slept in. Oh, my lady, Tamworthy and the footmen had to break down the door of the study.'

'Do you mean he had locked himself in his study?'

'Yes, my lady. Tamworthy says as how nobody could have got in and so he must have shot himself, my lady.'

Emma shook her head in a dazed way. 'Oh, no, Austin, he would never do that.'

'My lady, you are white and trembling. Please do not go downstairs. Please let me put you to bed.'

'No, I must find out what has happened.'

When she was dressed, Emma walked down the stairs to the main hall, where a small group of men were standing. There was a magistrate, a constable, a Bow Street runner and a doctor.

The magistrate walked forward to meet her. 'Lady Wright,' he said, and his eyes were hard and calculating. 'It is my sad duty to accuse you of the murder of your husband, Sir Benjamin Wright.'

Emma felt as if someone had punched her over the heart. She swayed for a moment and looked as if she would faint, but thrust Austin aside, who had rushed to her to support her.

'Why on earth do you say such a monstrous thing?' demanded Emma.

The magistrate signalled to the constable, who walked across the hall and held open the door to the library which was across the hall from the study. 'In here, Lady Wright,' said the magistrate. 'I am Sir Henry Biggs, magistrate at Bow Street.'

Emma walked in and sat down in a high carved chair in the middle of the room.

'Now,' said the magistrate, Sir Henry. 'The facts are these. Your husband was found shot through the heart. The murder was done with his own pistol. The pistol was lying on the floor near the door beside a fan that one of the maidservants has identified as your own. The door was locked, but I assume you have a key to the study.'

Emma shook her head. 'He would not allow either myself or any of the servants to have a key. I could not have shot him, Sir Henry, for I was locked in my bedchamber all night.'

'Get that butler here,' snapped the magistrate.

Tamworthy came in. He was the quintessential English butler, fat, with a large, white, heavy face and small, shrewd eyes. 'Tamworthy is devoted to me,' Sir Benjamin had often bragged.

'See here, Tamworthy,' said Sir Henry. 'Lady Wright says she was locked in her bedchamber last night and neither she nor any of you were allowed a key to Sir Benjamin's study.'

Tamworthy's bright little eyes in his large white face rested briefly on Emma. Emma shrank a little in her chair. She remembered threatening to kill Sir Benjamin only the night before.

The butler cleared his throat and said pompously, 'That is right, Sir Henry. I had instructions to see that my lady was locked in her room. Sir Benjamin took the decanter of brandy into the study and locked the door behind him. He had given instructions he was not to be disturbed. I heard a shot during the night, but Sir Benjamin had an abnormal fear of burglars and when he was in his cups, he would often fire his pistol.'

'This is most odd,' said the magistrate testily. 'Why was Lady Wright to be locked in her room?'

'Sir Benjamin said he was going to whip my lady before us servants in the hall in the morning.'

'Be careful what you say, man! Sir Benjamin was a most respected politician. I find all this hard to believe.'

Tamworthy took a deep breath. 'I tell the truth. Although Sir Benjamin's behaviour was worse than usual, he was in the way of abusing my lady shamefully. Led her a dog's life,' said Tamworthy with sudden passion.

His little eyes rested on Emma, and she was startled to see concern and affection in them.

The magistrate swung round to face Emma. 'That fan of yours, my lady. We must find out how it got there. Did you go into the study at any time?'

'I could not,' said Emma, beginning to feel as if she were living in a nightmare. 'How could I? I was locked in my room.'

Sir Henry signalled to the Bow Street runner. 'Show her the fan.'

Emma looked at it in bewilderment. It was the one she had carried to the ball the night before. It was a large one of blue and gold silk with ivory sticks. 'I attended the ball at the French ambassador's last night,' she said. 'I was carrying that fan. I cannot remember if I brought it home or left it in the ballroom.'

'Think!'

Emma half closed her eyes. The ballroom. Dancing in the arms of the Comte Saint-Juste, swaying to the music, the blurred faces of the watchers, the feeling of elation and happiness all floated through her dazed mind. 'I cannot remember,' she said. 'I cannot!' She buried her face in her hands.

And then she heard the magistrate say to

Tamworthy, 'You say Sir Benjamin treated Lady Wright badly. Did you at any time hear Lady Wright utter any threats against Sir Benjamin's life?'

Emma went rigid. Her own voice seemed to sound in her ears. *You monster! I could kill you!*

'No, sir,' she heard Tamworthy say. 'My lady was all that a good and obedient wife should be.'

The magistrate stared at him for a long moment. Then he said, 'Get the other servants in here.'

Emma kept her hands over her face. She heard the shuffle of feet as the staff filed into the room, and then there was a long silence.

'Now, hear me,' began Sir Henry after what had seemed like a lifetime to Emma, 'your good master has been foully murdered. You must answer this question honestly. I ask you all . . . at any time did any one of you hear Lady Wright threaten her husband *in any way*?'

Emma took her hands slowly down from her face. They were all looking at her, all those servants she had assumed to be so devoted to Sir Benjamin. They were looking at her, all of them, with a steady kindness and sympathy. The housekeeper, Mrs Chumley, elected herself spokeswoman. 'I think I speak for all of us, sir,' she said, 'when I say that my lady has been all that is kind and dutiful and patient.'

The magistrate dismissed them angrily. Only Austin insisted on staying, standing at attention behind her mistress's chair.

'It is all most odd,' he said grimly. 'You may retire, my lady. We shall summon you if we need you.'

Emma rose to leave, but her legs were weak and she clung to the arm of the chair for support. Austin put a strong arm about her mistress's waist and supported her from the room.

The servants were standing in the hall. They drew aside to let Emma and Austin past. As she mounted the stairs, she heard Tamworthy telling them to return to their duties.

All day long Emma sat in her bedchamber, numb with shock and guilt. She felt she had willed her husband's murder. For so long she had dreamed of being free of him, and now she was, but in such a macabre and sinister way.

And then toward evening she heard a high, commanding voice from outside. 'I demand to see Lady Wright and I will not be stopped. She is in need of friends.'

Emma let out a stifled little cry of relief. She recognized that voice – Matilda, Duchess of Hadshire. She opened her bedroom door and called to the servants, 'Let Her Grace attend me.'

Matilda, followed by Annabelle, Mrs Carruthers, entered the room.

The duchess was a small, dainty woman with hair so fair it was almost white. She looked like a Dresden figurine. Annabelle was tall and willowy with thick brown curls, large grey eyes, and a generous mouth.

To their questions, Emma falteringly outlined what had happened.

'So someone shot the old devil and tried to have you hanged for the murder,' said Matilda, whose forthright manner belied the fragility of her appearance. 'If it were not for the fact that the murderer tried to put the blame on you, I would wish him well.'

'Matilda!'

'There is no denying it, Emma. Your husband was a brute, and you are better off without him. What happens now?'

'I think there will be an inquest and then I must make arrangements to take . . . to take the body back to Upper Tipton for burial.'

'And then you had better return to London, dearest Emma,' said Annabelle.

'To the Season! T'would not be fitting.'

'But *we* are here and you will have need of friends.'

'I have my family to support me,' said Emma quietly. 'And the servants have been so kind. They are so loyal. I never imagined they would stand by me the way they have.'

Matilda and Annabelle exchanged glances. The news of Sir Benjamin's murder had spread through fashionable London like wildfire. The gossips had gleefully described how Lady Wright had danced like an angel in the arms of the Comte Saint-Juste and how her furious husband had marched her from the ball. Everyone seemed so very sure that Emma had shot him. But Emma looked so pale and miserable that neither had the heart to tell her of the wicked gossip.

After they had left Emma's house, Matilda and Annabelle discussed possible plans to travel with Emma to the country. 'For I have a feeling that she will need our support there as much as here,' said Matilda.

The duchess's glittering town carriage bore her home to her husband's palatial mansion in Grosvenor Square. She walked into the rich silence of the house and handed her gloves and walking cane to the butler and asked if her husband was at home. Hearing he was in the Yellow Saloon, she made her way up the curving flight of stairs to the first floor. She stood for a moment with her hand on the doorknob and then, squaring her shoulders, she opened the door and walked in.

Her husband, the tenth Duke of Hadshire, was standing in front of the looking glass that hung over the fireplace, adjusting his cravat.

'Good day, Hadshire,' said Matilda.

He held up one long, thin, almost transparent hand for silence, and Matilda waited with impatience as he studied his cravat and finally tweaked a pleat into place.

The duke was a collector of objets d'art, and he had added Matilda to his collection. Her fragile daintiness had roused his collector's zeal when he had first seen her at a country assembly. Her parents were of the gentry, not very rich, but comfortably off. Like Emma's parents, they, too, had a large family and were delighted at the prospect of such a glittering marriage for their eldest daughter. And so the duke was given Matilda's hand in marriage, and he felt the same thrill at taking her away from the church as he did when he bought a beautiful piece of china at an auction.

He was a tall, thin man, not ill-favoured, with large black eyes, a thin, straight nose, and a small, pretty mouth. The shoulders and chest of his coats were padded with buckram, and he wore false calves under his stockings. He was fastidious to a fault. He had quickly found a fatal flaw in Matilda. Despite her prettiness, she had a tough, almost masculine mind and a distressingly direct manner. It was as if his rare piece of china had proved to have a crack in it. He could not regulate her to the basement, and so, as he put it to himself, he made 'the best of a bad job'. So long as Matilda was dressed exquisitely in the latest fashions and did not try to converse with him on any subject that might be regarded as serious, he was able to tolerate her. They had been married for three years and had slept together as man and wife on only two occasions.

He swung round. 'You may speak,' he said.

'My friend, Lady Wright, is in distress,' said Matilda in that irritatingly strong and commanding voice of hers. 'Sir Benjamin has been murdered, shot through the heart in his locked study. It is a mystery how the murderer got in. Emma's fan was found on the floor near the body, and Sir Benjamin was shot with his own pistol, which he kept loaded in the desk. Fortunately, Sir Benjamin had commanded the servants to lock her in her bedchamber last night or she would most certainly have been charged with his murder. I would like to travel to the country with her and be of support to her during the funeral.'

The duke took out a snuffbox and with maddening deliberation helped himself to a delicate pinch. Then he said, 'No, you may not go. I have heard all about the murder from Rougemont.' Rougemont was the duke's valet and henchman. 'A most noisy and distasteful affair. You will have nothing more to do with Lady Wright. That is final.'

'Look, here . . .' began Matilda wrathfully. The duke held up his hand for silence.

'That is all,' he said coldly. 'You may leave.'

Matilda glared at him in frustration. At that moment she envied Emma the devotion of her servants. The duke's servants were all hand picked by the duke. She had not even been allowed to choose her own maid. And Rougemont, with his brutal looks and veiled insolence, frightened her. The duke had threatened before that if she disobeyed him, then he would send Rougemont to 'guard' her until she came to her senses.

'I wish someone would shoot *you*,' Matilda thought, as she turned and ran from the room.

In a less fashionable quarter of the town, Annabelle, Mrs Carruthers, was faring no better. The handsome ruin that was her husband shouted that they were not going to give up one social engagement of the Season simply because she wanted to dance attendance on a murderess.

* * *

A week later Emma stood in the churchyard in a thin drizzle as her husband's coffin was lowered into the grave. She had never felt more alone in her life. Sir Benjamin's relatives were there in force, his brother and sister and their children, and various cousins. The coroner in London had returned a verdict of murder by person or persons unknown and the interest in Emma had died down to a certain extent, but here, in the country, where Sir Benjamin had been so much admired, she felt she had been tried and found guilty. What her parents and brothers and sisters thought of the murder she did not know, except she did realize that she was a great embarrassment to them. Her younger sister, Jane, had just become engaged to Mr Worthing, a local gentleman, and they feared 'Emma's disgrace' might make Mr Worthing cry off.

But there was no outright hostility until after the reading of the will. It was a simple will. Sir Benjamin had left everything to his wife. But the size of his fortune drew gasps from everyone. As the outraged and disappointed relatives rose after the reading of the will to take their leave, Sir Benjamin's sister, Mrs Trowbridge, rounded on Emma. 'Murderess!' she cried, and was led weeping from the room.

To Emma's distress, her own mother and father said hurriedly that they must also take their leave. Emma had hoped they would stay with her for a little.

'It is better we go,' said her father, looking anywhere and everywhere except at his daughter. 'This is a bad business, Emma. Your husband was the finest man that ever breathed. A sad loss.'

'My husband', said Emma in a thin voice, 'was a tyrant and a monster.'

'Hush, dear,' said her mother, appalled. 'You must not talk so until the cloud over you has lifted. I would return to town if I were you, my love. Your presence here is making life awkward for poor little Jane.'

Emma looked at her mother's frightened, worried face and tried to remember just one occasion where her mother had hugged her or shown her any affection, and could not.

'I am now a rich woman,' she said bitterly. 'You can have anything you want.'

'Well, now, Emma,' said her father, dropping his voice to a whisper in case any of Sir Benjamin's relatives might have returned and been listening at the door, 'it would not be fitting. We are comfortable enough as it is. Leave things for a little, my dear. How Londonized you look! The country must seem tedious to you now.'

'Father, I am in need of love and support,' begged Emma. 'You know I did not kill my husband.'

'Yes, dear,' said her mother. 'But people do talk so, and poor little Jane. What if Mr Worthing should cry off!'

Emma sighed. 'Very well, you may go.' She sat down wearily and rested her head on her hand.

Then she felt a touch on her shoulder and looked up. Her mother's eyes were swimming with tears. 'Have courage, darling,' she said. Her voice dropped to a whisper. 'Forgive us. We are not very brave . . .'

Emma sat very still until she heard the door close, and then she began to cry. Matilda and Annabelle had sent sorrowful letters to Emma to say their husbands had forbidden them to have anything to do with her. Emma cried because she felt alone in the world, because she felt guilty for having hated her husband so much, and because the stigma of murderess was clinging to her.

Her parents appeared to have had a change of heart, for on the following day they sent their carriage with a request that she should live with them until she felt stronger.

Thanking God for this unexpected support, Emma packed up and moved into her parents' home. But her family was shy and awkward with her and obviously wished she had not come. For Emma was cut by everyone in the village. When she went out driving with her parents, some louts shouted, 'Murderess', and threw stones at the carriage and Emma's mother had strong hysterics.

And then Jane's Mr Worthing broke off the engagement, leaving no one in any doubt that it was because of Emma. 'Under the circumstances,' he wrote, 'you can hardly expect me to ally my name with that of yours.'

It was the last straw. Past crying, Emma grimly sent for the lawyers and settled a handsome dowry on Jane and on her other remaining unmarried sister and asked for a large sum of money to be paid to her parents.

Then she told her servants she would be returning to town, and as she left the village of Upper Tipton, she felt it would be many years before she could bear to return.

Shrouded in black, she entered her town house and saw to the unpacking of the trunks. The study door had been repaired, and the door was closed. Emma did not think she could bear even to look inside that room.

'Perhaps we should travel, my lady,' said Austin brightly as she shook out dresses and hung them away.

'Travel, Austin? I am weary enough from travelling as it is.'

'Might be cheery, seeing all them foreign parts,' said Austin. 'You know, my lady, we'd be away from anyone what knows us.'

'I know what you mean, Austin,' said Emma. Then she stood still and said, 'Who murdered Sir Benjamin, Austin? In all the shock and misery, I have overlooked that main question. No, not overlooked it exactly. How could I? But now, being back here, it has struck me with a great force. Someone shot him, Austin. Someone who tried to have me blamed for his murder.'

'It's them Irish,' sniffed Austin. 'Them with their shootings and bombs. Cunning devils. They probably came down the chimney.'

'I don't think it was anybody Irish,' said Emma. 'Indeed, I had heard Sir Benjamin speak most strongly on the tyranny of the English in Ireland. When the Duke of Wellington said that there could never be peace in Ireland unless Protestant and Catholic children were educated at the same schools, he supported him. Sir Benjamin had no enemies.'

'None that you know of, my lady,' said Austin. 'People are cruel, my lady. Believe me, after a week in London you'll be glad to take your old Austin's advice and travel.'

And Emma very nearly did. She had vaguely hoped to be able to meet either Annabelle or Matilda at some function, but she was invited nowhere, and when she went driving in the park, she was shunned.

She bought some books on Italy and began to dream of sunny skies and the friendly faces of people who had never heard of the murder of Sir Benjamin Wright.

And then one afternoon at the end of the following week when she was sitting in the drawing room, fighting with a black depression that was making her feel perpetually exhausted, Tamworthy brought up a card on a silver salver.

'A gentleman to see you, my lady,' he said.

Emma read the card. *The Comte Saint-Juste* was inscribed on it in curly script. It had one corner turned down to show that he had called in person. Emma remembered that waltz with shame. How could she have lost her senses in such a way? How could she have performed that solo dance with him and started tongues wagging?

'Tell the comte I am not at home,' she said wearily.

Tamworthy bowed. She heard his footsteps going down the stairs, the sound of a conversation, then rapid steps on the stairs, and the comte strolled into the drawing room followed by a much-flustered Tamworthy. 'Milord would not take no for an answer,' said Tamworthy.

The comte smiled and bowed low. 'I will take only a few moments of your time, Lady Wright.'

He had swept off his hat, and the sun shining in the window glinted on his golden hair. He seemed to bring life and colour into the room.

'Very well, Tamworthy,' said Emma. 'You may leave us. Pray be seated, Monsieur le Comte.'

He sat down gracefully and said, 'I have only just returned to town. Sad news.'

'Yes, shocking,' said Emma wearily.

'Who murdered your husband, my lady?'

'Have you not heard the gossip?' demanded Emma bitterly. 'I am supposed to have flown through a locked door on my broomstick and shot him through the heart.'

'That is because you are so very beautiful, *vous voyez*. Had you been Friday-faced, no one would have credited you with sinister motives. But me, I am intrigued. Your husband was a Tory. He spoke passionately on all sorts of causes that did not mean very much to anyone. At one time he wished Britain to take back the colonies of America by force, but that did not rouse any ire in anyone. There is too much sympathy for the Americans on both sides of the House. He wished fox hunting to be taxed. Ah, that *did* cause near apoplexy in some members but was soon forgotten. In other words, Sir Benjamin was a typical Member of Parliament – choleric and quite mad.'

'My husband appears to have commanded a great deal of respect, and yet you call him mad!' exclaimed Emma.

'Now, the gossips also say that you were locked in your room the night of the murder because your husband wished to have the pleasure of whipping you in front of his servants in the morning. Of course, the malicious say that the servants were in your pay, or, rather, were promised a bonus when Sir Benjamin's fortune passed to you . . .'

'Monstrous!'

'Ah, yes, but malicious gossip always is. On the other hand, dear lady, a totally sane man does not behave thus.'

Emma twisted a handkerchief in her hands. 'Sir Benjamin was incensed because I danced with you.'

'Perhaps not because you precisely danced with me but because you had the temerity to look as if you were enjoying it, *hein?* But we must set to work. Lead me to this mysterious study and we will begin our search for the murderer.'

'You are kind, milord, to concern yourself, but

I am so very tired and . . . and I would like to be alone.'

'Of course you would,' said the comte, 'but to do what? To sit in isolation and then find escape only in sleep?'

'Why should you wish to help me?' asked Emma wearily.

'Because it amuses me. Courage, milady. *En avant!*'

She could almost feel the force of his personality, of his energy, which seemed to charge the very air about her like one of Dr Galvani's electric machines. 'Very well,' she said weakly.

Tamworthy unlocked the study door, bowed and left. Emma wondered what the butler thought of this frivolous visitor, and would have been surprised had she known that Tamworthy, after his stately progress through the green baize door at the back of the hall, leapt down the back stairs like a gazelle to tell the other servants that that Frenchie was the best medicine my lady could possibly have.

Emma looked nervously around the study. The comte pottered about, studying the lock of the door, which had been repaired, the shutters at the windows, the clusters of bells hanging on their thin wires to deter burglars, the thick curtains, and the catches on the windows. He opened the shutters, drew back the curtains, unlocked the windows, and raised them to let fresh air into the room.

'Now,' he said, 'where was your husband when he was found?'

'He was seated there – behind his desk,' said Emma.

'And the fan?'

'Lying on this side of the door.'

'And the pistol?'

'Lying on the floor beside it.'

'*Tiens!* Have you considered that the murderer must have known your husband very well?'

'Why do you say that?'

'Was there any sign of a struggle, any sign of Sir Benjamin trying to save himself?'

'No.'

'And whoever it was may have known Sir Benjamin's habits. Why did the servants not come running at the sound of the pistol shot? He was not discovered until the morning.'

'My husband, when he was in his cups, fired off his pistol because he often thought he heard burglars. The servants had been told he was not to be disturbed. They assumed he was drunk.'

The comte knelt down and peered up the chimney. 'No one could have arrived or escaped that way.' He rose to his feet. 'I must ask you this, was there a woman in his life – a mistress?'

'Oh, no,' sighed Emma. 'Sometimes I even hoped . . .' Her voice trailed away.

'You hoped he would take one to give you some peace,' mocked the comte. 'Now, we will be businesslike.'

Half amused, half exasperated, Emma watched him take a notebook and lead pencil from his pocket. 'What are the names of his friends?' asked the comte.

Emma frowned in concentration. 'He did not appear to have friends, only acquaintances, other Members of Parliament. Let me see, so many came to call on social occasions. He did not have one close friend.'

'Then let us search this desk. Did he have a secretary?'

'Yes, Mr Tocknell. But Mr Tocknell has an office in Westminster and hardly ever came here. My husband preferred to write his own speeches.'

The comte began to search through the drawers of the desk. It was a large leather-topped desk with three drawers on either side. The drawers revealed bills and parts of speeches, but no diary or papers that could give one clue to the identity of Sir Benjamin's murderer.

The comte sat down in the chair behind the desk and sighed. 'The fan!' he exclaimed, sitting up straight. 'The servants must have been involved. How did your fan come to be here?'

'I don't know,' snapped Emma. 'I had it at the French ambassador's ball. I do not remember whether I left it there or brought it home.'

He half closed his eyes. 'Let me think. I held you in my arms. We waltzed. You were wearing diamonds and blue silk. Your gloves were white. I am holding your hand as we waltz and your other hand is holding your skirt. Do you carry your fan in your right hand or your left?'

'The right.'

The comte smiled with satisfaction. 'Now we are getting somewhere. You were not carrying your fan when we danced, but you did have it when we were sitting together. *Alors*, when you rose to waltz, you must have dropped it. You did not notice, for my charm had naturally bewildered you . . .'

'You are impertinent, sir!'

'Do not interrupt. Yes, someone must have found it. Perhaps that someone did not mean to shoot Sir Benjamin at that time but had arranged to meet him during the night. So . . . everyone here goes to bed and you are locked in your room. The murderer arrives at a prearranged time. Sir Benjamin lets him in. Words pass. Sir Benjamin falls dead. The murderer remembers the fan and throws it on the floor. The wife will be suspected and may hang. You did inherit your husband's money, did you not?'

'Yes, but I . . .'

'All of it?'

'Yes, Monsieur le Comte.'

'Was there much of it?'

Emma's eyes became hard. 'You go too far. I must point out that–'

'Don't be missish,' he said in a cool voice. 'How much?'

Emma told him.

He let out a low whistle. 'What about Sir Benjamin's relatives. Did not they hope to inherit?'

'He has a brother and sister, and, yes, they were most upset. His sister accused me of being a murderess. I was going to settle some money on them, but I . . . I . . . I could not bear to have any dealings with them.'

'So if you hang for your husband's murder, the money goes to the family.'

'I do not think it is quite so simple. Perhaps it would go to the Crown.'

'Aha, but let us imagine another scene. You are in prison and shortly about to hang. You receive a sympathetic visit from, say, the sister. You make your will in her favour, *non*? And . . .'

'No,' said Emma, shaking her head. 'His sister was quite genuine in her accusation. She is comfortably off. I do not think she was furious simply because I inherited all the money. I was not aware Sir Benjamin was so very rich, and now that I remember the faces of his family at the reading of the will, I am sure they did not know either.'

'Pity. But money is the root of most murders. Does this desk have a secret drawer?'

'I do not know,' said Emma. 'It doesn't appear to be that kind of desk. I mean, it doesn't have pigeonholes or anything.'

He got down on his knees and went under the desk and began tapping busily. 'The only way to make sure is to saw this desk up,' he said at last, rising again to his feet and smiling at Emma.

He rang the bell.

'Pray do not ring for my servants without asking my permission,' said Emma stiffly.

He did not pay any attention to her, but smiled on

Tamworthy, who answered his summons, and said cheerfully, 'I wish you to fetch me a saw. I am going to saw up Sir Benjamin's desk and look for a secret drawer. What is your name?'

'Tamworthy, my lord.'

'Very good, Tamworthy. It is up to us to find out who murdered Sir Benjamin.'

'His lordship's efforts to clear my name are most commendable,' said Emma coldly, 'but sawing up this desk is ridiculous.'

Tamworthy's shrewd eyes rested briefly on his mistress's angry, flushed, and very alive face, and said coaxingly, 'It's a nasty old desk with bad memories, my lady. I was going to ask your permission to get rid of it. And we do have a saw, and t'would only take a minute.'

'Very well,' said Emma, capitulating. 'But all you will have for your pains is a heap of firewood.'

They're like schoolboys, thought Emma as a footman and the kitchen boy set to sawing the desk apart while Tamworthy watched with interest and the comte leapt from one side to the other of them as he supervised the operation.

'No, no, my friends,' said the comte. 'You make the task too difficult. Take the drawers out first!'

The men did as they were told and then continued to saw, and the comte whistled under his breath.

'Look at the mess,' exclaimed Emma, 'and all for nothing!'

'Wait!' said the comte. 'There is something there. Stop sawing!'

Suddenly interested, Emma walked forward. He was poking about among shattered pieces of desk.

'*Voilà!*' he said triumphantly, holding up a small, fat, leatherbound diary. There *was* a concealed drawer. It was cunningly hidden at the back of the bottom drawer on the left-hand side.

'Now we shall find out what Sir Benjamin was so eager to conceal!'

THREE

The comte sat down in a chair beside the shattered desk and opened the book. Emma stood behind him and read the entries over his shoulder. They were few and far between and in the form of cryptic reminders – meet S. at Lombard coffee house, meet J. at Brookes's, and so on. The comte read on.

'There is nothing of interest there,' said Emma, disappointed.

He held up a hand for silence and continued to turn the pages. 'The appointments are only during the Season,' he said at last. 'And there is nothing written down for the night of the murder. I shall go back to last Season and read the entries again. There must be something.'

Emma felt a great weariness descend on her again. She dismissed the servants and began to pace the room. The comte continued to scrutinize the pages, unconcerned.

'Here!' he said suddenly, stabbing a long finger down one page. Emma came back to stand behind him. 'You see?' he said. 'Last year, May second, "Meet H. in Yellow Saloon at Harvey House ball, midnight."'

'So all that appears to be, Monsieur le Comte,' said Emma impatiently, 'is another innocent reminder.'

'Perhaps. But if we find out who H. is then we will find out the name of one person he knew well, the one person important enough to meet at midnight. Look at it like this. If it were just an ordinary person in his life, some acquaintance with whom he wished to speak, why not just walk up to him at the ball and draw him aside? I shall ask Lord Harvey.'

'And do you think Lord Harvey will remember who it was visited the Yellow Saloon at midnight almost a year ago?' demanded Emma.

'Action is what you need, Lady Wright,' said the comte briskly. 'Put on your bonnet and pelisse and we shall go to the Harveys'.'

'I do not see the point in going,' said Emma. 'Besides, I am in mourning, or had you forgot?'

'It is perfectly *convenable* for me to escort a respectable widow. What would you do otherwise? Sit and brood? The clue to the murder lies outside this house. Unless you suspect one of the servants.'

Emma gave a little shiver. Her mind ranged over the staff, and she shook her head.

'Then come, Lady Wright. The sun is shining and we have a mystery to solve.'

Emma was about to protest when Tamworthy entered again with a note in the shape of a cocked hat on a silver salver. She opened it. It was a short message from Mrs Trumpington, asking Lady Wright to call for tea on the following day. Emma was delighted. It was at Mrs Trumpington's that she had first met Matilda and Annabelle. A little of the black misery at her heart began to ease. All at once it seemed better to go with the comte rather than return to her own company and her own despair.

'I shall not be very long, Monsieur le Comte,' said Emma.

'I am glad to see you going out and about, my lady,' said Austin, her monkey-like face crinkling up in delight.

'I must be mad,' said Emma as Austin helped her into a black silk pelisse and placed a black straw bonnet with a wide brim on her glossy curls. 'This French comte is determined to find out who killed Sir Benjamin.'

'Well, someone has to,' exclaimed Austin.

Downstairs, the comte surveyed Tamworthy and asked slowly, 'Would you say your late master was a good man?'

The butler look uncomfortable. 'Sir Benjamin had his moods, milord. Very tetchy he could be on occasion.'

'Yes, whipping his wife before the servants could be described as tetchy.'

'He did not actually perform that act, milord.'

'No, but he would have, had not some obliging person shot him dead. Now, listen, if we are to find out about Sir Benjamin's possible enemies, we have to go about in society. By "we", I mean Lady Wright and myself. I can make inquiries on my own, but, you see, Lady Wright will go into a decline if she does not have a purpose in life. I need your help.'

'Anything I can do, milord. But what *can* I or any of the other servants do?'

'You can start by attempting to restore Lady Wright's character. You must forget a servant's loyalty to a late master and gossip about his tempers and his cruelty to Lady Wright. You must say that she is horrified that his murderer is left free to walk the streets, and despite Sir Benjamin's appalling treatment of her, she is determined to see justice done. You will say that *I* told you that the Prince Regent himself is interested in the plight of the poor, maligned widow. Do you think you can do that?'

A broad smile creased Tamworthy's fat face. 'I shall be delighted. The Prince Regent himself! Wait until the other servants hear that!'

Oh, well, thought the comte ruefully, there were so many lies about the Prince Regent, one more would not matter.

He stood up as Emma entered the room. Despite her black hat, black gown and black pelisse, she looked very beautiful.

As she allowed the comte to help her into his open carriage, she had a feeling that eyes were staring at her. In this she was right. Her servants were peering through chinks in the closed curtains to see her leave.

'Bless her,' said Mrs Chumley. 'He's a handsome man, the comte.'

'But a foreigner,' pointed out Tamworthy severely. 'He will do very well for the moment, however, to keep my lady amused. Now, Mrs Chumley, call all the servants down to the hall. Milord has a plan to save Lady Wright's reputation.'

'It might be a good idea to redecorate,' said the comte as he tooled his carriage expertly through the traffic.

'Redecorate what?' asked Emma, surprised.

'Your town house. Mausoleum of a place, all dark walls, and paintings in need of cleaning. Enough to give anyone the megrims.'

'I think murder is depressing me and not paint or the lack of it,' said Emma severely.

'Surroundings are very important,' the comte pointed out. 'Who was responsible for the furnishings? Sir Benjamin's ancestors?'

'No, he bought that house just before our marriage. I believe he bought the furnishings with the house. He did say something about it having been rented out for the Season by the previous owner.'

'Flowers,' said the comte cheerfully. 'As a start you need plenty of vases of flowers, bright, cheerful flowers. Can you not persuade some relatives to stay with you? Are your parents alive?'

'Yes, milord. But I have brothers and sisters and

my parents must stay in the country and look to their care. I . . . I have two very good friends in London, but their husbands have forbidden them to have anything to do with me.'

'Perhaps things will soon change. How did your husband gain his income? He does not own much land, does he?'

'Only a few acres let to a farmer. I believe all the money was well invested. Consuls, stocks and bonds.'

'Here we are.' The comte halted the carriage outside an imposing double-fronted house in Berkeley Square. He took out his card case, extracted a card, turned down one corner, and handed it to his tiger, who was perched on the backstrap. The servant nipped up the steps and performed a loud tattoo with the door knocker. The louder the flurry of knocks, the greater the consequence of the visitor. The comte's tiger, a small, wizened Frenchman who looked like a retired jockey, was a master of the art.

The door opened, the tiger presented the card and came back to hold the reins while the comte helped Emma to alight.

Emma held back a little. 'I have a feeling we are about to be most dreadfully snubbed,' she whispered. The comte's blue eyes glinted down at her.

'But you are with me,' he said. 'And no one dares to snub me.'

When they were ushered into a saloon on the ground floor of the Harveys' house, and when Lord Harvey rose to meet them and his pale eyes rested for a moment on Emma's face, Emma had a feeling that he was well and truly shocked at her appearance in his home.

To Emma's surprise, the comte began to chatter inanely about operas and plays, gossip and trivia. But the cold look left Lord Harvey's eyes and he began to relax. He was a tall, thin man with the severe face of a Scottish minister which belied the fact that he hardly ever thought of anything more serious than his dogs or his debts. His dogs, King Charles spaniels all five of them, lay about the room, sleeping off a heavy meal.

'What a rattle you are, Saint-Juste,' said Lord Harvey at last. He smoothed down the folds of his shot-silk banyan – that dressing gown beloved of the aristocracy for undress – and added, 'But Lady Wright has not had a chance to say anything. My deepest sympathy on your recent bereavement.'

Before Emma could reply, the comte said quickly, 'Ah, but milady cannot begin to mourn properly while the murderer of her husband goes free.'

'Indeed!' said Lord Harvey, and with all the direct callousness of his breed, went on. 'I thought she topped our Member of Parliament herself.'

Emma coloured furiously, but the comte said easily, 'Fie, for shame, Harvey. You of all people to be so behind with the gossip. Lady Wright could not have murdered her husband because she was locked in her bedchamber on her husband's instructions. He wished to beat her before his servants in the morning. A horsewhip, I believe. Quite medieval.'

'Come now,' said Lord Harvey. 'Sir Benjamin was a typically stolid Englishman. I appreciate your defence of the divinely beautiful Lady Wright, Saint-Juste, but you cannot make me believe Sir Benjamin was a Gothic monster.'

'In the same way you could not believe a word against our friend Mr Palliser? Yet, if you remember, it was well and truly proved that he beat his poor wife to death, as well as having very odd tastes in amusement. You English!' The comte spread his hands in a Gallic gesture. 'All country sports and clean living on the outside and the sins of the fall of Rome on the inside. And so we are all going to find the murderer of Sir Benjamin, *hein*? And with your help.'

'My help? My dear fellow, I am hardly intimate with the bourgeoisie, although I may occasionally invite a few of them to a party. I barely knew the man.'

The comte leaned forward. 'You gave a ball on May second last year. In his diary Sir Benjamin has made a note that he planned to meet a certain H. in the Yellow Saloon at midnight.'

'Much as I would like to help,' said Lord Harvey in bored accents, 'I cannot possibly remember who was in the Yellow Saloon at midnight one year ago. Come now. I do remember Sir Benjamin was present at the ball. He played cards all evening and did not once join the dancers.'

'Well, that's a start. With whom was he playing cards?'

Lord Harvey put a long, thin finger up to his brow. 'Let me see. The game was whist and the stakes were high. Sir Benjamin always played deep but never seemed to lose, even when he was in his cups. There was James Henderson, Lord Fletcher, Lord Framley . . . yes, I am sure that was it. I remember, you see, because of the high stakes and because there were a great many people watching them play. Sir Benjamin won.'

The comte rose to his feet. 'I shall ask them if he left the card table at midnight. I am most obliged to you, Harvey.'

'*De rien.* I must apologize for the fact that my wife is still in bed. Otherwise I am sure she would be delighted to receive you.' Lord Harvey gave Emma a cold look, and she knew he really meant that if his wife knew that that murderess, Emma Wright, was in her house, then she would never have thought for one moment of putting in an appearance.

'So that is that,' said the comte as they drove off. 'But I did not expect this to be easy. Still, we have made a start. Now, did you sleep with your husband?'

'My lord!'

'I mean, did he have his own bedchamber?'

'Yes, but . . .'

'So we will now go and search it. No, do not protest. What would you do without me? Sink into apathy.'

Emma looked at his handsome profile, at his long, muscular legs in leather breeches and top boots braced against the spatter board of the carriage, and said quietly, 'Why should you interest yourself in my welfare, milord?'

'Because it amuses me,' he said again.

Emma felt a stabbing pain at her heart. He would soon tire of the chase and then she would be left alone again. Austin was right. She should travel.

When they arrived outside Emma's town house, the comte looked up at the windows. The curtains were tightly drawn and the blinds were down. Even the study curtains, which the comte had drawn back, were once more closed again.

'The funeral is over,' he said. 'There is no need to live in perpetual twilight. Tell the servants to open all the curtains and raise the blinds.'

Emma nodded, suddenly too tired and depressed to argue with this man who looked on her and the murder of her husband as an amusement.

But as the servants ran from room to room, opening the curtains and lifting the blinds and opening up the windows, she felt a lift at her heart as sunlight flooded the rooms. She ushered the comte into her husband's bedchamber, looking about her with that old familiar feeling of fear. His heavy presence still dominated the room. His shaving things were still laid out on the toilet table, and the air smelled of the cologne he liked to wear.

She sank down into a chair and watched as the comte went through every drawer and cupboard. He even opened up the wig cupboard and shook out the wigs. 'Was Sir Benjamin bald?' he asked over his shoulder. 'Three of the best nut-brown wigs.'

'No, he was old-fashioned,' said Emma. 'He wore his own hair cropped short under one of his wigs.'

The comte turned his attention to the toilet table. 'A vain man,' he murmured. 'The best scented soap, pomades and pomatums, creams and lotions. And all the bottles topped with gold stoppers. Musk pastels for bad breath. Ugh! False teeth. Waterloo teeth. I am amazed he was not buried with them.'

'An inexpensive spare set,' said Emma. Waterloo teeth were so called because women had been sent over to the battlefield to extract the best teeth from the corpses to supply the dentists of London.

The comte turned his attention to a large William and Mary wardrobe in the corner. He opened the doors and began to go carefully through the pockets of Sir Benjamin's coats. 'Snuffbox,' muttered the comte. 'Handkerchiefs, quizzing glass . . . nothing much here. Where is his jewel box?'

'On that shelf on top of the wardrobe,' said Emma.

He reached up and brought down a heavy japanned box. 'Unlocked. Good,' he said, placing it on the bed and raising the lid. 'Fine jewels, rings, stickpins, watch chains, seals. We lift the top out and what have we? More rings and seals and fobs and . . . aha, a pack of cards.' He sat down on the bed and extracted the cards from the pack and then ran the tips of his fingers over the surfaces.

His eyes glinted with excitement as he held out a card to Emma. '*Regardez*,' he said triumphantly. 'Marked cards!'

'I don't see anything wrong with them,' said Emma.

'Run your fingers very lightly over the surface. Do you feel them? Little pin pricks, my dear Lady Wright.'

He scrabbled in the bottom of the box again and then lifted out a pair of dice. He weighed them in his hand and then crouched down on the floor and rolled them, and then again, and again.

'We are trying to find out the identity of my husband's murderer,' said Emma crossly, 'and all you can do is play dice.'

He leapt to his feet. 'You widgeon, you beautiful widgeon,' he cried. He held out the dice. 'Do you know what we have here? A bale of bard cinque deuces, a bale of flat fice aces, a bale of fulhams, a bale of demies, a bale of contraries . . . in other words, false dice. Oh, heavens above and all the angels bless me, your esteemed Member of Parliament, that rock of society, that so-worthy husband, was a cardsharp. Now, *there's* a motive for murder. What delightful perfidy. What a villain. Let us look at the magic box again. Any secret compartments? Yes, the bottom tray lifts out and what have we? Papers, by all that's holy.' He unrolled them and then cast a quick glance at Emma and rolled them back up again.

'What is in the papers?' demanded Emma.

'Not papers. Illustrations of a naughty nature, Lady Wright. Enough to bring the blush to the most hardened cheek. Oh, my poor Lady Wright.'

His voice was warm with sympathy and his eyes, kind. 'You are not even surprised,' he said gently.

'What horrors of the bedchamber lie locked behind that beautiful face of yours. Come, you will serve me tea and then I shall go out and about and find the three men who were playing cards with your husband at the Harveys' ball.'

Emma was suddenly shy of him. His personality filled the room. He belonged to a London world she had only visited but had never been part of, a world of frivolity and gaiety and ease.

As they sat over the teacups, he did not talk anymore about the murder, but rattled on gaily about his life in society and how he planned to take part in a curricle race on the morrow. Then he turned his attention to the drawing room. The walls were mud-coloured, the original wallpaper having been varnished over. Various bad and dark and dirty paintings were hung around the room, and the furniture was heavy and carved and ugly, upholstered in dark purple velvet. The curtains at the window were also of purple velvet. A William and Mary marquetry longcase clock by Edward Burgis with a square-topped hood and a yellow face stared down into the room and sonorously ticked off the seconds. The fireplace was a massive marble affair without decoration and surmounted by a large greenish-looking glass.

'You could start with this room,' he said. 'A little brightness – even a little – would make so much difference.' He put down his teacup with a little click. 'Now I must go off on the hunt.'

Emma envied him as she stood a few moments

later at the window and watched him spring into the carriage, shouting something over his shoulder to his tiger that made the tiger laugh. He seemed so free of care.

But she was reluctant to return to her dismal thoughts. Not only was fresh air blowing through the house, but it was as if the comte had blown some fresh air into her mind. She rang for Mrs Chumley and told the housekeeper that she might consider redecorating the rooms of the house, starting with the drawing room. She went on a tour of the house. Downstairs, off the black-and-white-tiled hall, was the study, now locked again. Then there was the library, a small, sombre room with dull, uninteresting books behind glass cases. Beside the library was a saloon, smelling of disuse. Emma realized with a little shock that they had never entertained there during the Season. On the first floor was the drawing room, the Blue Saloon, although it was a uniform brown, and a little morning room, and next to that a dining room. On the second floor lay the bedrooms and, above them, the attics.

And then as she emerged into the hall again, it was to find Tamworthy and two footmen taking in bouquet after bouquet of flowers. There were early roses and tulips and great bunches of lilac. There were freesias from the Channel Islands and tubs and tubs of hothouse exotics. Their colours blazed in the dark hall and filled the air with a heady smell of perfume.

'Who sent these?' asked Emma, although she already knew the answer.

'Monsieur le Comte,' replied the butler. 'Dear me, I do not know where I shall find enough vases, my lady.'

'Buy all that is needed,' said Emma, suddenly lighthearted. She felt full of energy after her days and days of lethargic despair. 'And have the carriage brought round, Tamworthy. I must go to Sir Benjamin's lawyers. I do not even know how to make out a cheque at the bank!'

The comte was in luck. By sheer coincidence, Mr James Henderson, Lord Fletcher and Lord Framley were all in White's Club in St James's. They were just leaving the card room as he arrived, all looking very downcast. The comte wondered if some other cardsharp had just fleeced them.

He invited them to join him in a couple of bottles of burgundy, and they readily agreed. The comte had the reputation of being an amusing rattle. They sat down with him at a table in the coffee room and prepared to enjoy the comte's usual frivolous flow of conversation.

The comte prattled on happily while he covertly studied the three. Mr James Henderson was handsome in a very English way, tall, with good shoulders and a square face and very blonde hair and light-blue eyes fringed with fair lashes. He had resigned his commission after Waterloo and appeared to have substantial means. Lord Fletcher was a fribble. His thin brown hair was artistically curled, his face was whitened with blanc, and the palms of his hands stained pink with cochineal. He wore fixed gold spurs on his boots, and his coat was well padded with buckram at the shoulders so that he had the air of a man frozen in the middle of a shrug. Lord Framley had one of those heavy Hanoverian faces: pale bulbous eyes and thick lips and a short neck. He was carelessly dressed. His coat was covered with snuff and wine stains, and his linen was dirty.

The comte waited until they were at their ease and then said suddenly, 'Congratulate me, *mes amis*, I have a purpose in life at last.'

'Something serious, no doubt,' drawled Mr Henderson. 'A night with our latest opera comet, Madame Divine?'

'Oh, much more serious than that,' said the comte. He hitched his chair forward. 'I am going to discover who murdered Sir Benjamin Wright.'

This was met in dead silence. Three blank faces looked back at him.

Then Lord Framley gave a loud laugh. 'Haw, haw, haw,' he guffawed, slapping his fat thighs. 'You had us there for a minute. Stap me! T'was that wife of his. Everyone knows that.'

'Oh, no, they don't,' said the comte. 'Lady Wright was not arrested, and the reason she was not is that she was locked in her bedchamber all night. So you see, we have a murderer at large in society.'

'Probably some seedy burglar,' said Mr Henderson, stifling a yawn.

'I say,' yelped Lord Fletcher, 'it's as plain as day

that Lady Wright bribed the servants to say she was locked in her room. I heard that story.'

'But I have met the servants myself,' said the comte gently, 'and they are the soul of honour.'

'People say she's a witch,' said Lord Framley petulantly, 'and that's how she could get into that locked room. Anyway, why come to us?'

'You were playing cards with Sir Benjamin at the Harveys' ball during May last year. In his diary Sir Benjamin has one cryptic note. He was to meet a certain H. in the Yellow Saloon at midnight.'

'You have been at the playhouse too many times,' laughed Mr Henderson. 'Where is the Yellow Saloon anyway?'

The comte looked at him, almost comical in his dismay. 'I never think to ask the simplest questions,' he exclaimed.

'Well, I'll tell you,' said Lord Framley. 'It's on the ground floor, almost directly under the ballroom.'

'So, do you know who went there at midnight?'

Lord Fletcher's lips curled in a sneer. 'You expect us to remember what happened a year ago?'

'I thought the three of you might remember that particular evening. Sir Benjamin relieved you all of a great deal of money.'

'Stap me! If you ain't right,' said Lord Fletcher. 'And that's the last time I played with him. The man had the luck of the devil.'

The comte wondered whether to tell them that the late Sir Benjamin had been a cardsharp, but decided against it. Lady Wright would promptly be besieged by the half of London society demanding their money back if that story got around.

'So, how long did the three of you play?' pursued the comte.

They all looked at each other and then shook their heads. After a few more questions, the comte left, feeling depressed.

'You missed an amusing call,' said Lord Harvey to his wife. 'The Comte Saint-Juste.'

'You should have told me,' pouted his wife. 'Our comte is ever amusing.'

'Ah, but he brought Lady Wright with him. He is determined to clear her name.'

Lady Harvey looked at her husband in amazement. 'But she has been accused of nothing.'

'Except by society,' her husband pointed out. 'Saint-Juste has found a cryptic clue in Sir Benjamin's diary. Evidently, Sir Benjamin was to meet a certain fellow referred to as H. in our Yellow Saloon at midnight at our ball last year. As if anyone could remember who was there.'

'Absolutely ridiculous,' began his wife. 'I . . .' Then she let out a gurgle of laughter. 'But I can tell you who was there. Madame Beauregard and her latest amour in such a state. I opened the door to see if I had left my shawl there, you know, the Norfolk one, because Mrs Betty was most eager to see it, and there they were! I blushed all over and closed the door. And it must have been just about midnight.'

Lord Harvey laughed. 'We'd better tell the fellow

Comte Saint-Juste is hot on his trail. I shall probably see him this evening. What sport! Was not our comte himself interested in La Beauregard once? Murder, fiddle.'

'It is all a piece of folly,' said his wife. 'The comte cannot have formed a tendre for the pretty widow – Madame Beauregard is a more likely candidate. People call Lady Wright pretty – but how can they call a waxwork pretty!'

That evening, Emma fell asleep, a bouquet of flowers on a table beside her bed. But during the night she had a horrible dream. Her husband was not dead. It had all been a macabre joke. She was pulled from her room and dragged down to the hall to face that public beating. The comte was standing among the servants. He looked gay and debonair. 'What sport we are having!' he cried when he saw her.

'No!' screamed Emma, and woke with a start. With trembling fingers she turned up the wick of the oil lamp she kept lighted beside the bed.

The house was very still and quiet. A horseman rode past on the street outside. From far away came the voice of the watch calling the hour. She lay for a while trembling, reluctant to fall asleep again in case some other horrendous dream should be waiting for her. She picked up a book from the bedside table, determined to read for a little until she felt calmer.

And then she heard it.

A faint footfall on the stairs.

She swung her legs out of bed and wrapped

herself in a dressing gown. She crossed to the bell to ring for the servants and then hesitated. Her nerves must have been playing tricks with her hearing. She looked at the clock. Two in the morning. That was what the watch had been calling.

She lit a candle and, holding it aloft, softly opened the door and made her way along the corridor. It was the one way to cure her morbid fantasies, she thought. She would find the house empty apart from the sleeping servants.

The candlelight threw eerie shadows dancing up the walls. The eyes of a portrait suddenly seemed to glare at her out of the gloom. She reached the head of the stairs and raised the candle high.

Then she froze.

A black-masked figure was standing halfway up the stairs, his eyes glinting behind his mask.

He took a half step toward her, and Emma screamed and screamed and dropped the candle. She turned and blindly groped her way along the corridor, dived into her room, and slammed and locked the door. She closed her eyes, her hand at her heart as she heard the servants thudding up from the basement and down from the attics.

Then she heard Tamworthy's voice outside her door. 'Are you safe, my lady?'

She unlocked the door. 'There was a man on the stairs, Tamworthy,' she cried. 'Search the house.'

Tamworthy turned away and soon could be heard shouting out orders. Emma waited, her large eyes dilated with fear.

At long last Tamworthy returned. 'There was no sign of anyone,' he said reassuringly. 'My lady must have had a bad dream.'

In vain did Emma protest. The main door had been locked and bolted on the inside, just as the butler had left it after he had done his rounds.

She returned to her bedchamber and began to pace the floor. If only the comte were not going on that silly curricle race. *He* would believe her.

FOUR

As Emma drew on her gloves preparatory to going out to call on Mrs Trumpington the following day, she said to Tamworthy, 'Do you know where the Comte Saint-Juste resides?'

'It will be easy to find his direction,' the butler replied.

Emma pulled a letter from her reticule and handed it to him. 'See that this is delivered to the comte. I cannot have been imagining things. There was a man standing on the stairs last night.'

'But, my lady,' protested Tamworthy, 'we have searched every corner of the house. The front door was bolted and locked. Nothing has been taken–'

'Nonetheless,' Emma interrupted, 'take my letter to him just the same.'

Followed by Austin, she left the house and climbed into her carriage. *My carriage now*, thought

Emma. *Oh, how much I would enjoy all this wealth and freedom if I did not have this shadow of suspicion hanging over me.*

Mrs Trumpington was sitting in an armchair in the gloomy recesses of her drawing room when Emma was announced. She was a very old lady, distressingly smelly, but with quick, intelligent eyes in her wrinkled face.

'Forgive me for not rising to greet you, Lady Wright,' she said. 'My legs are weak. Now you must sit by me and tell me all your adventures.'

'I have not really had any adventures,' said Emma.

'Tush! Your husband murdered in cold blood and you thought to have done it! Now, *that* is an adventure. I do so envy you. Nothing so exciting as that ever happens to *me*.'

'And I pray it never does,' sighed Emma. 'I hate living in this atmosphere of suspicion–' She broke off as she heard sounds from the hall of other arrivals.

The door opened and Matilda, Duchess of Hadshire, and Annabelle, Mrs Carruthers, tripped in.

Emma ran to meet them, hands outstretched. 'I never thought to see either of you again,' she cried.

'And that is what we told Mrs Trumpington,' said Matilda with a laugh. 'And the dear lady arranged this meeting.'

'And how do you both go on?' demanded Emma when they were all seated around the tea table.

Matilda shrugged. 'As usual,' she said bitterly. 'But you are our prime concern. Tell us everything that has happened.'

And so Emma told them about the comte's help, about the mysterious visitor during the night, about the cryptic messages in her husband's diary.

'I know the Comte Saint-Juste,' Matilda said, with a sly look at Emma. 'Vastly handsome, my dear, and a fribbler.'

Although *fribbler* was usually shortened to *fribble*, Hugh Walpole had invented the word. A fribbler was, he explained, a man who could take serious things lightly, but who at the same time delighted in taking frivolous things seriously.

The fribble, or fribbler, was very much part of the Regency world; it was an age when the dilettante enthusiastically sought out rare pictures with the same vigour as the country squire and his parson pursued the fox.

'I think every woman in London has given up hope of ensnaring him,' commented Annabelle. 'A hardened flirt, Emma.'

'I am grateful to the comte for his help,' said Emma primly.

There was a slight snore from the corner. Mrs Trumpington had apparently fallen asleep.

'What is it like,' asked Matilda, lowering her voice, 'to be free? You are now a rich and independent widow.'

'I feel guilty,' said Emma in a small, tired voice. 'I did not murder Sir Benjamin, but I wished him dead so many times that I almost feel I *had* killed him. People look at me *so*. I have thought and thought, until I am weary, of who could have possibly wanted to kill him. He was a brutish man in private but in public he was all that was respectable . . . apart from one thing.' She told them about the marked cards and the loaded dice.

'Then that is that!' cried Annabelle. 'Matilda and I will ask around discreetly and find out the names of those he fleeced the worst. My husband,' she added bitterly, 'must know the name of every hardened gambler and cardsharp in town.'

'But be careful what you put about,' admonished Matilda. 'For if society knows Sir Benjamin was a cheat, then you will have all sorts who never even sat down with him at the card table claiming to have a lost fortunes and expecting you, Emma, to make reparation.'

'Which reminds me,' said Emma, turning to Annabelle, 'I am very rich, extremely rich, and I know, dear Annabelle, you are often . . . er . . . embarrassed. Please let me be your banker.'

Annabelle shook her head. 'It would be throwing good money after bad. My husband would take the money, but he would never pay off any of the duns or even his tailor. Any money goes straight on the gaming table. He borrows and borrows, from friends and relatives, but he is never at home when they come calling for their money, and I . . . I am so *weary* of it all.'

There was a sympathetic silence. Then Annabelle gave a brittle laugh. 'When we find your murderer, Emma, pay him to kill my husband. T'would be worth every penny.'

'Shame!' said old Mrs Trumpington, startling the three. 'The Lord above can hear you.'

Annabelle was unabashed. 'I have prayed and prayed, Mrs Trumpington, for relief from my plight, but He does not concern Himself with such as I.'

'His eye is on the sparrow,' said Mrs Trumpington.

'And a lot of good that does us,' snapped Matilda, and then flushed as Emma and Annabelle gave her shocked looks. Such outright blasphemy was going too far.

Emma told them again about the message about H., who was to meet Sir Benjamin in the Yellow Saloon at the Harveys' ball, but Matilda said that no doubt H. was merely someone who wanted to settle a gambling debt in private. This seemed such an eminently sensible idea that Emma began to rapidly lose hope of ever being able to clear her name.

The Comte Saint-Juste won the curricle race and accepted the prize of a Limoges snuffbox and a dozen bottles of champagne. He opened the champagne on the spot and passed it around and then sat back in his carriage with his friend, Mr Peter 'Jolly' Simpson. Jolly had earned his nickname by being perpetually good-humoured. He was an odd friend for the elegant and clever comte to have. He was as English as roast beef with a round red face like a country squire and a thick stocky body and slovenly clothes.

'Prime race,' he said after drinking a bumper of champagne down to the dregs and wiping his mouth on his cuff.

The comte sipped his own glass, his eyes wandering absentmindedly over the English countryside. He suddenly felt alien, a foreigner in a foreign land, and longed for the fields and poplars of his native France and to hear his own language. The company about him conversed in a cant so broad as to be almost incomprehensible. His mind slid back to the murder of Sir Benjamin.

'You have heard of the murder in society, Jolly?'

'Oh, you mean Sir Benjamin,' said Jolly easily. 'Good riddance.'

'Now, why do you say, "good riddance"? Everyone else seems to think he was a sterling fellow married to a wicked wife who murdered him.'

'I notice things,' said Jolly simply. 'The ladies don't really like dancing with me and I don't like to gamble – well, not cards or dice – and so I've got time to watch people at balls. Lady Wright always looked miserable to me, and once I heard him saying several very nasty things to her. If she did it, then good luck to her.'

'But she could not have done it, *mon ami*, for she was locked in her bedchamber all night. And whatever devil did it managed to get through two locked doors. How do you explain that?'

Jolly yawned, put a plump hand under his waistcoat, and scratched his chest.

'Must have had a key,' he said lazily.

The comte looked at him in surprise. 'Of course,' he began, and then his face fell. 'But the main door was bolted on the inside.'

'Then,' said Jolly reasonably, 'he probably had a key to the back door. I've noticed that people put locks and bolts and chains on their front doors and leave the back one with only a flimsy lock. I say, look at Lord Harvey over there. He's trying to balance a bottle on his nose.'

'You are a very intelligent fellow,' said the comte slowly.

Jolly looked pleased but puzzled. 'Well, I notice things,' he said. 'Don't suppose you'd have noticed Harvey balancing that bottle on his nose if I hadn't pointed it out.'

The comte eased himself down from his carriage and strolled over to Lord Harvey's curricle. Lord Harvey had stopped his balancing act and was opening a fresh bottle. 'Splendid race, Saint-Juste,' he said when he saw the comte. The comte leaned against the side of the curricle and looked up at him. 'You haven't managed to remember who it was visited your Yellow Saloon at midnight last year?'

Lord Harvey gave a tipsy laugh. 'Me wife does, but I ain't telling you. If a fellow wants a bit of fun with a lady, there's no call to go spreading the gossip around.'

The comte's eyes sharpened. 'Aha! Give me one name, Harvey, or I shall begin to think the mysterious H. was yourself.'

'Not I, Saint-Juste. But my lips are sealed. Promised m'wife not to breathe a word.'

In vain did the comte protest that he was perhaps shielding a murderer. Lord Harvey only laughed drunkenly and said he was merely shielding a philanderer.

The comte returned to his carriage, climbed in and picked up the reins. 'Hey, where are we going?' cried Jolly, hanging on to his hat as the comte urged his team forward.

'I am going to pay an amorous call on Lady Harvey,' said the comte.

'Bit long in the tooth, what?' commented Jolly, trying to pour champagne into his glass despite the lurching of the carriage.

A smile curled the comte's lips, but he did not reply and concentrated on the road ahead. He set Jolly down in Piccadilly and made his way to the Harveys'.

He was in luck. Lady Harvey was at home. She was a plump matron in her forties with a face like a pug. When she had ordered wine and cakes for her unexpected visitor, she asked him if there was any particular reason for his call.

'The only reason,' said the comte, smiling into her eyes, 'is because I know your husband is not here.'

'La!' Lady Harvey fanned herself vigourously. 'You are funning, Monsieur le Comte.'

'Not I,' he said lightly. 'I have long admired your charm of manner and the wittiness of your speech.'

Lady Harvey regarded the handsome comte with a look of dazed gratitude. Unlike many society matrons, she would never consider being unfaithful to her husband, but it was glorious to be so flattered, and by such a personable bachelor.

'You must not tease me,' she said. 'I am a faithful

wife. It is your French blood. The French are ever fickle.'

'Come, my lady, tell me the name of just one of my compatriots whom you would describe as flighty.'

'I was not thinking of any *man*.'

'Odso! A lady, then. Come . . . tell.'

'No, Monsieur le Comte.' Lady Harvey closed her fan and rapped him painfully on the knuckles with the ivory sticks. 'I abhor gossip.'

This the comte knew to be untrue but, then, London's chief gossips were always the ones who claimed to loathe tittle-tattle.

He wondered briefly if some fickle Frenchwoman could have anything to do with the Yellow Saloon. He chatted easily of other things, subtly flattering her until she was nearly purring.

'I am surprised you should pay such attention to me when my husband is convinced you are enamoured of Lady Wright.'

'Not I. She is too cold; she lacks animation. But she did not murder her husband, and I would dearly like to find out who did.'

'Why?'

'It amuses me.'

'As I amuse you?'

'Lady of my heart, do not be so cruel. I called on your husband with Lady Wright because I wanted to know if he remembered who had been in your Yellow Saloon at midnight on the night of your ball last year. You see, Sir Benjamin was to meet someone there, and that is all I have to go on.'

Lady Harvey laughed. 'Oh, I know who was there at midnight, but I am not going to tell you. It could ruin a reputation.'

'But it might save Lady Wright's reputation.'

Lady Harvey pouted. 'I have no interest in that little bourgeoise.'

'Nor I,' he said, his hand on his heart. 'Dear lady, smile on me once more. Has anyone ever told you that your eyes are like deep pools of water lit by glints of sunlight?'

He talked on in this fashion until he heard the sound of a carriage stopping outside the house.

'Harvey!' he cried. 'I must take my leave.' He bent over her hand and placed a burning kiss on the back of it. 'Who was in the Yellow Saloon,' he whispered.

She blushed and hesitated and then gave a little shrug. 'You will not tell anyone?'

'Light of my life, give me one name.'

'It was Madame Beauregard and–'

She broke off in confusion as her husband reeled into the room.

'What ho, Comte!' shouted Lord Harvey. 'Just leaving? Stay and we will continue to celebrate your victory.'

The comte managed to turn a laughing face to Lord Harvey and then a guilty one to his wife – *a deliciously guilty look*, she thought.

'Unfortunately I have an appointment with two bottles of burgundy elsewhere,' he said lightly.

He made them both an elaborate bow and left.

'What a character,' said Lord Harvey with a grin.

His wife was glad he did not ask why the comte had chosen to call when the master of the house was not at home and then was piqued that he obviously assumed the call to be innocent.

The comte made his way to his home, turning over in his mind what he knew of Madame Beauregard. She had appeared on the London scene two years earlier. She said she and her husband had escaped the perils of Napoleon's France and had been staying for some time in the English countryside. She was from Normandy and a genuine blonde with large pale-blue eyes and a voluptuous figure. There was no scandal attached to her name. Her husband, Jacques Beauregard, was a small, sallow man who said little and did not often appear in society. The couple appeared to be rich. That was the sum total of his knowledge of them.

His servant handed him Emma's letter and he read it carefully. He bathed and changed and then made his way to Emma's house.

As usual, she was wearing black, and he had a sudden longing to see her out of mourning. He listened carefully as she described the events of the night and then surprised her by asking to see any back entrance to the house.

She led him down the stairs and through the servants' hall and kitchen, scullery, and stillroom to a door that led into a weedy garden. It had two thin glass panels and a sturdy lock. The door showed no signs of having been forced.

He opened the door and went into the garden, scanning the ground carefully and then going over to the wall at the end of the garden. 'What is on the other side of the garden wall?' he asked.

'The Bear and Ragged Staff Mews,' said Emma. 'The carriage is kept there.'

'There is no door from the garden to the mews, I see.'

'No, when I need the carriage, the servants walk round by Chapel Street and then along the mews to order it.'

'Stay here,' said the comte. 'I will let you know if there is a way up to the wall on the other side.'

He made his way out of the house and went around to the mews, counting the carriage houses as he went. Then he stopped. The grooms and coachmen lived above and the carriages and horses were kept underneath. But just behind where he judged Emma's house to be, a narrow, thin alley ran between the mews cottages up to a garden wall. He made his way along it and called loudly, 'Lady Wright?' and heard her voice answering, 'Yes!'

For his evening call on Emma, he had donned his best corbeau-coloured coat, knee breeches and white silk stockings with gold clocks. He looked down at his dress ruefully and then shrugged and began to scale the wall. Emma looked up, startled, as the comte's head appeared over the top of the high wall.

He hauled himself up astride the top of the wall and looked down at her. She was standing by a mossy sundial, and a shaft of pale evening sunlight lit up the beauty of her glossy black hair and the slim pliancy of her figure. She looked young and lost and alone, and he felt an unfamiliar tug at his heart. He scrambled down the wall into the garden, produced an enormous lace-edged handkerchief, and began to fastidiously brush down his clothes with all the self-absorption of a sleek cat at its toilet. 'Faugh!' he said. 'You have a dirty wall.'

Emma began to laugh. 'Milord, I am not responsible for the state of my garden wall,' she said. Her eyes were very deep blue, almost black, and he studied her as curiously as he studied his own reactions to her. Emma suddenly blushed and looked away, and he collected himself with an effort.

'Do you have the address of Mr Tocknell, Sir Benjamin's secretary?'

'No, but Tamworthy knows his direction.'

'*Bien.* I will call on him and then return here and sit in this uncomfortable garden for the night and see if our caller chooses to return.'

'You are very good, but . . . but what if something should happen to you?'

He took her hand in his and said softly, 'And that would distress you?'

'Of course.' Emma tugged her hand away.

'Nothing will happen to me,' he said. 'I shall see to that. You are not going out this evening?'

'No,' said Emma bitterly. 'I am in mourning and in disgrace, so I do not receive invitations.' Then her face cleared and she told him of her visit to

Mrs Trumpington and of her reunion with her two friends who had promised to help.

'Then tell them to find out all they can about a certain Madame Beauregard. She was present in the Yellow Saloon at midnight with, I assume, a certain gentleman. I gather from Lady Harvey's attitude that they were an amorous couple, but we must be sure. Can you remember if your husband ever met this Frenchwoman?'

Emma shook her head and he sighed. 'Every road seems to lead nowhere at all. Still, I shall try the secretary.'

Tamworthy said that Mr Tocknell, the secretary, lived in 10 Paster Street, Bloomsbury. The comte wondered whether to return home and change, trying to persuade himself that he would need warmer clothing for a night's watch in Emma's garden and ignoring the mocking little voice in his head that was whispering that he wanted to look his best in front of Emma. He firmly decided that a change of clothes was definitely needed, and that took some time, and then he was delayed by a visit from Jolly, who listened with interest to the latest developments.

Jolly took himself off to the club, leaving the comte to finish his toilet. He was asked on all sides about the Comte Saint-Juste's investigation of the death of Sir Benjamin, for the gossip had spread rapidly, and seeing no need for secrecy, Jolly cheerfully told them of the investigations to date.

It was dark when the comte set out for Bloomsbury,

cursing his own vanity and yet hoping illogically that Emma would admire his new waistcoat, which was embroidered with pink carnations.

Mr Tocknell's lodgings proved to be in a tall building divided up into small apartments. A bewildering line of white china bellpulls like organ stops ornamented the side of the front door. But which bellpull would jangle on its wire and call Mr Tocknell? He chose one and pulled hard. A window shot up above his head and a woman in an enormous linen cap looked down at him as he backed onto the street to get a better view.

'Mr Tocknell!' called the comte.

'Six,' shouted the woman, and slammed down the window.

The comte pulled the bell that had a neat '6' pencilled beside it on the whitewash. No reply. He pulled again. Obviously Mr Tocknell was out for the night.

He half turned away but was assailed by a strange feeling of foreboding.

He jerked the bell he had pulled first, and again the woman in the linen cap appeared at the window.

'Can you let me in?' called the comte. 'I fear my friend, Mr Tocknell, has been taken ill. He was poorly earlier today.' The woman did not reply, but she did not slam down the window although her head disappeared inside. He mounted the steps and stood next to the door. Then slowly it swung open, the woman having obviously operated a lever from the landing above.

There was a dim oil lamp on the first landing. He made his way up the stairs until he came to a door with a number six painted on it. He knocked loudly, listening to the quality of the silence. He had a strange feeling that the whole building was holding its breath.

He slowly put out his hand and turned the doorknob, and to his surprise the door swung open.

He edged his way cautiously inside. The little hall was pitch-black. Feeling his way, he came to another door and pushed it open. The flickering light of the parish lamp outside the window illuminated a corner of the room where there was a table with a candle in a flat stick. He lit the candle and held it aloft – and nearly dropped it.

From a ham hook in the ceiling swung the lifeless body of what could only be Mr Tocknell, a pathetic figure in neat brown clothes and buckled shoes, his feet turned in pathetically like the feet of a hung game bird.

And then there came an eldritch screech from the doorway – the woman in the white cap and a burly man behind her with a cudgel. 'Foreigner, murderer,' howled the woman when she had stopped screaming. People were beginning to crowd in behind her. Voices were calling for the watch, for the constable, for the militia.

In vain did the comte try to explain. No one was going to let him leave until the authorities arrived. He began to worry about Emma. He glanced around the room, ignoring a volley of insults about frog eaters and murderers. The room had been ransacked. Books had been torn from the bookcases and ripped apart. The fire was not alight but the grate was full of charred paper, and a few sparks still glowed among the blackened mass.

I wonder if it is suicide, thought the comte, *or if someone knew I was coming here. Jolly! He was going to the club. Perhaps he talked.*

He held the candle high and his eyes narrowed. There were chairs overturned around the room, but no chair was lying where Mr Tocknell might have kicked it away had he killed himself. He studied the face of the dead man. There was a knot in the noose, placed cunningly under his right ear, which had caused his neck to break. His face looked remarkably peaceful.

The crowd at the door suddenly fell silent.

With relief the comte turned back to face the doorway – the forces of law and order had arrived.

Emma waited by the window of the drawing room, wondering what had happened to the comte. The maid, Austin, who had elected herself chaperone as Emma could not be left alone with a French comte all night, sat sleeping in an armchair in the corner of the room.

Down in the street below, carriages came and went from the other houses. Laughter came up to Emma's listening ears. It was another world to her, a world she had never known, a world of gaiety and freedom. The comte belonged in that world, not sitting in a weedy garden. He was probably now getting merry in some club or ballroom and had forgotten all about her. Two young ladies entered a carriage on the other side of the street. They were dressed in shockingly thin muslin, and they were very pretty.

Emma had bathed in rosewater and had pomaded her black hair until it shone with purple lights. She had put on her best black silk gown. She began to feel silly. The comte could have no interest in such as she.

The little French clock on the mantel chimed midnight, and Emma turned away from the window with a sigh. He would not come now. She would wake Austin and tell the poor woman to go to bed. *How faithful the servants are*, thought Emma, her eyes filling with tears. *I must find out from Tamworthy how much they are paid and give them more. Such loyalty should not go unrewarded.*

The scent from the comte's flowers filled the room, and Emma's heart filled with a strange yearning.

And then she heard a brisk tattoo on the street knocker and stood still.

She heard the door opening, Tamworthy's voice, and then a light step on the stairs.

Austin struggled awake and got to her feet.

'A million apologies, my lady,' said the comte. 'But what an evening I have had! Brandy, I pray you, and then you shall hear all.'

Emma rang the bell and ordered brandy. She noticed his face was pale and drawn and he had lost his usual air of insouciance.

'That is better,' said the comte when he had drained a full glass, which Tamworthy had poured for him. 'Now, I shall tell you all . . .'

He leaned forward in his chair and told the horrified Emma of the death of the secretary. 'I would have been here earlier,' he finished, 'had I not thought it my duty to point out that Tocknell had all the appearance of a man who had been drugged and then slung up on that hook. I am a Frenchman and immediately became prime suspect despite my help. Whoever murdered Tocknell was desperately searching and destroying his papers.'

Emma then asked the question the comte had been hoping she would not. 'It is almost as if someone knew you were going to call on the secretary,' she said. 'But how can that be?'

He sighed. 'While I was changing my clothes I talked to a friend of mine about my proposed visit. He then left for his club. I am afraid he must have talked. I did not counsel him to remain silent, did not even think of it. But we are wasting time. I should be at my post in the garden.'

'No,' said Emma sharply. 'Not tonight. You have suffered a great shock.'

A wicked twinkle lit up his eyes. 'Ah, you care a little for my welfare, I see. That will sustain me through the night.' And despite Emma's protests, he insisted on going ahead with his watch.

Emma found she could not sleep, and so she arose quietly and dressed again without summoning her maid. She went down to the drawing room and stood at the back window, which overlooked the garden, and peered down into the darkness.

A small moon was racing through the clouds. The comte lay sprawled in an easy chair that the servants had placed for his comfort in a corner of the garden; she could just see the shine of the buckles on his shoes in the pale, fitful light. He was very still, and she wondered whether he had fallen asleep.

The clock on the mantel tinkled out two strokes. Emma half turned away from the window and then turned back again. Perhaps she should go down to the garden and make sure he was not asleep. It was dangerous to fall asleep when at any moment . . .

Her eyes sharpened. Surely there was a slight movement at the top of the wall. She backed behind the shelter of the curtain and looked around it. A hand and a leg appeared over the wall. She glanced down at the comte. He was motionless, or appeared to be.

Her heart began to hammer. If she shouted for the servants, the man would escape. Sir Benjamin's sword stood in the corner. He had worn it when he had been a major in a volunteer regiment that used to drill in Hyde Park in the days when an invasion from France seemed imminent. Emma seized it and hauled the sword from its scabbard and ran down the stairs, down and down to the back door. She opened it gently and moved silently into the garden.

A small snore reached her ears. Amid all her distress and acute fear, Emma could still feel a stab of impatience at the sleeping comte. She peered into the blackness. The moon was behind the clouds and the garden seemed very still. And then a black figure detached itself from the blackness at the end of the garden.

Throughout her short life, Emma had been as quiet and biddable and submissive as any lady of her age was supposed to be. But suddenly she was consumed with a hot rage. All her treatment at Sir Benjamin's hands, all her frustration at the unfairness of the suspicions about her, all her fear for the safety of the comte, hit her with force.

'Awake!' she shouted. 'The murderer is here!'

And waving the clumsy sword, she ran toward the intruder. He was masked but his eyes glittered strangely. He turned and darted to the wall. Emma raised the sword above her head and then swung it in a great arc. The heavy sword flew from her hand and impaled itself in the garden wall between the bricks, and the intruder scaled the wall like a cat and disappeared over the other side.

'You silly widgeon,' said a cross French accent in her ear. 'We could have had him.'

Emma swung around and faced the comte.

'You!' she said passionately. '*We* could have had him? *You*, sir, were asleep.'

'I was only feigning sleep.'

'I heard you *snore*.'

'I was feigning snores. I saw him arrive and decided to wait until he reached the kitchen door and then spring on him, and then you came out, waving that sword. Now we shall never know who he was and it's all your fault.'

'It is not my fault!' panted Emma, and then burst into tears.

'Now then,' said the comte, gathering her in his arms. 'I did not mean to be so harsh. Shhh! All is well.'

He freed one hand, took out a handkerchief, and mopped her face. 'This will never do. I had better go home and get my traps and stay here.'

'Y-you c-cannot,' sobbed Emma. 'It is not respectable.'

'I shall find you a chaperone. Do not cry, Lady Wright, or I shall kiss you.'

Emma broke free from him and blew her nose on his handkerchief as Tamworthy erupted into the garden, brandishing a blunderbuss and followed by the other half-dressed and frightened servants.

Jolly was awakened by his valet and told that the Comte Saint-Juste had arrived and demanded to see him.

He squinted blearily at the clock. 'Four in the morning,' he howled. 'The fellow must be foxed. Oh, send him up.'

Jolly eyed his elegant friend with disfavour. 'I say, I hope you've got a good reason for waking a chap up.'

'A very good reason,' said the comte, sitting down on the edge of the bed. He told the amazed Jolly about the murder of the secretary and about the scene in the garden. 'And what I want to know, Jolly, is did you tell anyone at the club that I was going to call on that secretary?'

Jolly groaned. 'I told just about everybody. Damme, you didn't tell me it was a state secret.'

'Framley, Fletcher, and Henderson . . . were they among those you told?'

Jolly scratched his head. 'I think so. Lots of chaps there.'

'Well, in future, *mon ami*, take everything I say as a state secret. Now . . . Lady Wright cannot be left unprotected, and so I am going to stay with her.'

'That'll set the tabbies talking!'

'Not if she has a respectable chaperone. Come, Jolly, like all good English gentlemen, you've probably got a spinster aunt, a poor relation tucked away somewhere.'

Jolly groaned. 'Only you Frenchies would expect a fellow to think at this ungodly hour.' His fat face creased up like a baby's as he thought hard. Then his face cleared. 'O'course, there's Cousin Agatha. Miss Tippet. She's staying with m'mother and mother would be deuced . . .'

His voice trailed away. He had been about to say his mother would be deuced glad to get rid of her. He himself though Miss Tippet a poor sort of female, but Jolly shared all the contempt and dislike of men of his age for unmarried ladies without dowries.

'Excellent. How soon can you fetch her?'

'Tomorrow. Anytime. Only go away and leave me alone.'

'Is she in the country?'

'No, right here in town. Now, go away . . .'

'Take her to Lady Wright's by tomorrow evening. Good night, Jolly. You look awful, and I have seen enough horrors for one night!'

FIVE

Emma awoke early the next morning with a rare feeling of anticipation. The terrible weight of depression that had plagued her days since her marriage to Sir Benjamin seemed to have lifted. For the first time in her life she could do what she wanted – within reason. There was no longer a fight for privacy with her brothers and sisters in the crowded home in which she had been brought up, nor was there now the dread of Sir Benjamin's choleric temper.

She summoned Tamworthy and asked to see a list of the servants' wages. She found they were all being paid provincial rather than London wages, and low ones at that, and told the gratified butler that she was raising all their salaries to the level of West End London servants. Then she cut short his effusive thanks by asking him to summon a locksmith to change the lock on the back door and an ironmonger to put bars on the glass panels.

Emma then called for her carriage and asked the coachman to take her to St James's Park. She had arranged a meeting with Matilda and Annabelle, who had both said they could contrive to escape their homes in the morning before their husbands woke up, the London fashionables not waking until two in the afternoon.

It was a warm, grey morning with a damp mist curling around the lime trees that bordered the narrow strip of water in the park. The cannons that had been placed there to make a last stand against an invasion by Napoleon gleamed wetly in the pale light. Matilda arrived first and then Annabelle. The ladies all climbed into Matilda's coach.

Emma told them of the latest developments and of the murder of the secretary.

'It will soon be in the newspapers,' said Matilda. 'Then surely society cannot go on blaming you for the murder of your husband.'

'So someone has a key to your back door!' interrupted Annabelle, who had been thinking of the earlier part of Emma's narrative, which dealt with the happenings in the garden. 'Have you changed the lock?'

'My butler is getting it changed this morning,' said Emma. 'But did the murderer get the key from Sir Benjamin, or did he come to the house when we were in the country and examine the lock to find out which type of key would fit it?'

Annabelle shook her head. 'No, don't you see? He must have a key to the study as well. It must have been someone with whom Sir Benjamin had private dealings. He gave him the keys so that he could slip into the house unnoticed in the middle of the night when you and the servants had gone to bed.'

'He was always most insistent that neither I nor the servants went anywhere near the hall in the middle of the night,' said Emma slowly. 'I remember once I decided to go to the kitchen and make myself some tea when I could not sleep. I got only as far as the hall – it was about three in the morning – and Sir Benjamin suddenly came out of his study and ranted and raved at me for disobeying orders.' She sighed. 'But as he ranted and raved about so many things, I did not find it odd at the time. Oh, there is something else. The Comte Saint-Juste has said he will come and stay with me after he finds me a chaperone.'

'Oho!' teased Annabelle. 'Sits the wind in that quarter?'

But Matilda had gone very still. 'You look shocked, Matilda,' teased Annabelle.

'No, not shocked, only worried,' said Matilda. 'What, for example, if the comte should prove to be the murderer? What better way of finding any incriminating papers than to gain your confidence, Emma, and then go through the house at his leisure.'

Emma gave a shaky laugh. 'Tish, you will have me suspecting the whole of London. I am grateful to the comte for his help.'

'Has he formed a tendre for you?' asked Matilda

curiously. 'He seems to be going to an unconscionable amount of trouble on your behalf.'

Emma turned her face away and looked out at the dripping trees in the park. 'Of course not,' she said. 'He is like all fribbles – he takes his pleasures seriously. But he is my sole support at the moment. I miss *you*, my friends. Oh, I wish we did not have to meet in this underhand way.'

'There is something in the wind,' said Matilda. 'You may not remain ostracized for long. My lady's maid was chattering the other night about how it is the talk of the town about what an evil man Sir Benjamin was – treating his saintly wife so cruelly. And now, of course, with this other murder, surely suspicion will be lifted from you.'

But Emma, who did not know that her servants had been gossiping assiduously on her behalf on the comte's instructions, sadly shook her head. 'I do not think London society will ever accept me now,' she said. 'And I think the comte will soon tire of the game of hunting for the murderer.'

Annabelle glanced uneasily at the watch pinned to her bosom. 'I feel I must go,' she said. 'My husband lost more money last night and was drinking deep. He will be in a foul mood if he wakes up and finds me gone. Why did I ever marry him? Why did I ever marry at all?'

'It is our lot in life,' said Matilda sadly. 'Sold to the highest bidder. That is the way of the world.'

The three women hugged one another affectionately and then went on their separate ways.

Emma approached her home in Curzon Street with a nagging feeling of dread. She was tired, and the events of the night before struck her with force. Tamworthy was waiting for her with the news that the murder of the secretary was in some of the morning newspapers. Emma was amazed. In the country, the local newspaper was often months late with the news, let alone days. She decided to go back to bed and get some much-needed sleep, telling Tamworthy to rouse her if the comte should call.

She awoke at noon and rang for Austin to dress her. She went down to the drawing room and tried to read, tried to play the piano, but found she could not concentrate on anything. Fear dogged her thoughts. When the comte was present, it seemed to Emma that his very presence gave her hope.

The day wore on. The comte did not call, but, to her surprise, several members of society did and other left cards and invitations. Emma had become the latest curiosity. Her servants' gossip had done its work. Society was now prepared to believe her innocent and to secure the novelty of her presence at their parties.

By evening she had given up hope of seeing the comte again. Surely for such a dilettante as he, the novelty of the chase had palled.

The Comte Saint-Juste was being entertained by Madame Beauregard. He had waited in his carriage opposite her home in Manchester Square until he had seen her husband leave.

He explained the reason for his call. He said

he was weary of speaking in a foreign tongue and wished to converse with one of his own country-women, while all the while his lazy blue eyes surveyed Madame Beauregard, wondering if this beautiful creature could have anything to do with the death of Sir Benjamin.

And she *was* beautiful in a full-blown way. She had creamy skin and a high colour, corn-blonde hair, and very full, very red lips. Her plump figure was voluptuous and her elbows, of which she was very proud, daintily dimpled.

'I sympathize with you, my dear comte,' she said, leaning back against a satin-covered, red-and-white-striped sofa in a way that showed her snowy bosom in a low-cut gown to the best advantage. 'These English! Such clods. So heavy and ponderous in their conversation and cold in their amours.'

'And yet,' said the comte, 'they gave so many of our countrymen refuge from the Terror.'

'The Terror, the Terror,' she said with a shrug. 'I believe the tales to be grossly exaggerated. Seventeen thousand dead, they say. Impossible.'

'Not impossible, alas, madam. There are too many witnesses still alive to tell the tale of the massacres.'

The comte glanced around the well-appointed drawing room and at the rich hangings. Who were the Beauregards? And where did their money come from?

She was leaning toward him now. 'Tell me,' she said huskily, 'what is the *real* reason for this visit?'

'Your beauty, madam, draws me like a moth

to the candle flame,' said the comte, startled for a moment at his own lack of originality. But Madame Beauregard seemed to take it as her due. 'You forget, I am married,' she said, lowering her lashes.

'And I would you were not,' cried the comte. 'Pah! This English society wearies me. I long for my own country, my own countrymen. I long to see France strong again and no longer under the heel of these brutish conquerors.'

Now I have gone too far, he thought. *But I must gamble. I must fish. I must cast out lures and see which bait she will take.*

Her beautiful eyes narrowed a fraction. 'So the restoration of our monarchy does not please you?'

'What can a fat fool of a king do?' he exclaimed. 'Was all the suffering and bloodshed for nothing?'

'No,' she said in a low voice. 'It was for three things – equality, liberty and fraternity.'

The comte experienced a feeling of triumph. So Madame Beauregard was a Jacobin. His mind raced. So what connection could there be between this French lady and a respectable British politician? And then a voice in his head seemed to say, *But this respectable politician loved money so much that he marked the cards and loaded the dice.*

'France can be restored,' said Madame Beauregard urgently. 'There is a way . . .' Her voice trailed off and her blue eyes were suddenly shrewd. 'But we shall talk of lighter things. Why do you pay court to me when society knows you to be enamoured of Lady Wright?'

'Oh, Lady Wright,' he said casually. 'She amused me for a time, but I cannot strike sparks from a cold statue.'

'It is also said you are interested in finding out the murderer of Sir Benjamin Wright.'

The comte laughed. 'My dear lady, I have no interest whatsoever in who got rid of the old fool. It was a means to an end, you see. That interest is over.'

She patted the sofa beside her. 'Come and sit next to me, dear Comte,' she said, 'and tell me when you first became attracted to me . . .'

The comte left an hour later and climbed into his carriage, resisting the temptation to scrub with his handkerchief the lips she had so recently kissed. She might be watching him from the window. He had not asked what she had been doing in the Yellow Saloon that midnight; that would have been too clumsy. But he knew that Madame Beauregard longed for the escape and restoration of Napoleon.

Jolly was waiting in the library of the comte's house with a small, fat, bad-tempered-looking woman whom he introduced as his cousin, Miss Agatha Tippet.

'I trust Mr Simpson has explained matters to you, Miss Tippet,' said the comte. 'You are to chaperone Lady Wright. I am investigating the murder of her husband, and it is essential I move into her home in Curzon Street. But Lady Wright must be correctly chaperoned.'

'Does she keep a good kitchen?' asked Miss Tippet querulously.

'I have not dined there, Miss Tippet, but faults in the cuisine can be easily remedied.'

Miss Tippet had a short neck and one of those heavy, thick-lipped faces you see in Hogarth prints. 'I like my food,' she said still in that irritatingly cross voice. 'Mr Simpson has told me my duties, and I will take them seriously. While I am in residence, there has to be no . . . er . . . between you and Lady Wright.'

'You are in danger of being impertinent, Miss Tippet,' said the comte sharply, 'but rest assured, there will be no . . . er . . . at all. Now, I shall escort you to Curzon Street so that you may take up residence immediately. What is it, Jolly?' Mr Simpson was grimacing and winking.

'Excuse us a moment, coz,' said Jolly, and drew the comte from the room. When they were outside, Jolly said urgently, 'Are you sure you want the old quiz? She's as greedy as a pig and she's demanding a lot of money.'

'I'll pay her,' said the comte. 'I haven't the time to look for anyone else. With any luck, Lady Wright will need to endure her for only a short time.'

Had the comte brought Miss Tippet to her any earlier in the day, Emma might have refused her chaperonage. But when they arrived, darkness had fallen and Emma had been beginning to imagine murderers lurking in the dancing shadows thrown by the candle flames.

'For reasons I would like to keep to myself for the moment,' said the comte after he had introduced

Miss Tippet to Emma, 'I would not like it known that I am residing here. In fact, I shall only sleep here and be seen at my own home as much as possible.'

'I would like some supper,' interrupted Miss Tippet.

'Madam, you already ate supper,' said the comte.

'That was a little bite, nothing more,' said Miss Tippet. 'The only way I can face this unusual situation with equanimity is to eat to keep my spirits up.'

Emma rang the bell and ordered Tamworthy to serve Miss Tippet with supper in the dining room and felt relieved when that large lady eventually departed to take yet another evening meal, leaving the door pointedly open so that, as she put it, no . . . er . . . could take place in her absence.

'Horrible, isn't she?' said the comte with a grin. 'You shall not have to endure her company for very long.'

'Have you discovered something?' asked Emma.

'A little. But I will let you know as soon as I have something positive. You can rest easy tonight, Lady Wright. Have you a bedchamber prepared for me?'

'Yes, of course, and it has a window overlooking the garden. I have had callers today. It seems society has decided I did not kill my husband.'

'Excellent. There is no need to wear full mourning any longer, and it will do you good to get about a little. All men are not as your husband was. You are now a rich widow and can afford to pick and choose.'

'I shall never marry again,' said Emma firmly. 'I have found freedom and do not want to relinquish it.'

The couple looked at each other, suddenly feeling out of sorts. The comte wondered why he was wasting his time looking for murderers when the frivolities of life were so much more entertaining, and Emma thought he was a shallow-brained man who assumed marriage to be her only goal in life.

Miss Tippet returned, breathing heavily through her nose, and demanding permission to retire. Emma rose and said she would like to retire as well, and Tamworthy was summoned to show the comte to his room.

Emma felt sad and depressed as she lay in bed. The comte had been quiet and polite as he made his good-nights. His eyes had not held that teasing, mocking and caressing look that had so excited her senses. He did not care for her one whit, she thought miserably. Not that she wanted him to, of course. But it was very lowering to find he thought her unattractive.

When Emma arose the next morning, it was to find the comte had already left. Miss Tippet ate a solid breakfast of grilled kidneys, bacon, eggs, cold pheasant and toast, all washed down with a small beer.

She did not seem a very talkative lady. Emma wondered what she thought of her odd situation and then decided that Miss Tippet thought only of food and how much she could get of it.

The day was fine and sunny and the footmen had

rolled down the red-and-white-striped awnings over the windows. Emma felt restless, a dowdy black figure on this glorious day. She sent a footman to summon one of London's top dressmakers and then spent a happy hour going through magazines and fashion plates, choosing a new wardrobe.

This action seemed to have brought her to life. She told Miss Tippet to get ready to go out and sent for the carriage. They would drive in Hyde Park and look at the fashionables, and with luck she might meet Matilda and Annabelle.

With Austin she searched the contents of her closets until she found a dull blue silk carriage gown trimmed with black velvet, suitable for half mourning. She ripped the flowers from a shady bonnet and pinned a ribbon of black velvet around the crown. 'Now I look less like a crow,' she said to Austin as she twirled around in front of the long glass in her bedchamber.

Austin privately thought her mistress had never looked better. There was a flush of pink on Emma's cheeks and a sparkle in her blue eyes.

Miss Tippet grumbled under her breath as she climbed into the open carriage. She had been looking forward to an afternoon nap. She was wearing a fusty grey carriage dress that was strained to bursting point over her roly-poly body, and a coral necklace, her pride and joy, had disappeared into the folds of fat around her three chins. She wore a hard, flat, squarish hat impaled with a large pin ornamented with a carved ivory eagle.

Emma tried to make polite conversation as the coachman drove them sedately toward the park, but Miss Tippet answered only with mumbles and grunts.

To Emma's delight, a great many people smiled and bowed to her. It was almost possible to forget that the murderer of her husband was still at large and might strike again. Surely the secretary, Mr Tocknell, had simply committed suicide, and whoever it was who had killed her husband had been cheated by him at cards.

The most superb carriages and horses in England were on parade in the park, their occupants dressed in the finest silks and muslins and jewels.

And then she saw the Comte Saint-Juste. He was driving his curricle and talking to his companion, a ravishing blonde dressed in near-transparent pink muslin. She laughed at what he was saying and put a dimpled little hand on his arm.

Emma felt lost and alone and frightened. The comte had said that finding the murderer of her husband was merely an amusement. But she had not believed him. She had hoped . . . But she refused to allow herself to think what she had hoped. The comte did not see her. She called to the coachman to head for home, and then with relief she saw Annabelle and Matilda sharing a vis-à-vis approaching briskly in her direction. She called again to the coachman, this time to stop.

'You see, dear Emma,' cried Annabelle. 'You are fashionable again and it appears we are to be allowed to visit you.' She looked curiously at Miss Tippet, and Emma made the introductions.

'Miss Tippet is a relative of Mr Simpson, the Comte Saint-Juste's friend. The comte feels I need a chaperone.'

'Yes,' said Matilda doubtfully. She thought Miss Tippet a very depressing sort of chaperone. 'We saw the comte. What is he doing with Madame Beauregard?'

'Is that who she is?' said Emma airily. 'Probably one of his amours.'

Matilda said slowly, 'If she is, then it is odd. I do not remember our frivolous comte ever having set up a mistress, although he is a hardened flirt.'

'I thought the comte was in love with you,' said Annabelle. Emma threw a warning look in Miss Tippet's direction although Miss Tippet had extracted a bonbon from her reticule and was crunching with the slow satisfaction of a ruminating cow and seemed oblivious to everything else. 'Oh, here come three of my husband's gambling friends.'

Lord Framley, Lord Fletcher and Mr Henderson rode up and reined in beside them. They already knew Matilda, so Annabelle introduced Emma. While Lords Framley and Fletcher talked to Annabelle and Matilda, Mr Henderson said to Emma in a low voice, 'I am so sorry for all the distress and misery you must have endured over the death of your husband, Lady Wright. I knew him well.'

'I do not remember meeting you before, sir,' said

Emma, 'but, then, the only friends of my husband whom I met were Members of Parliament or ambassadors or diplomats.'

'I would I had met you a long time ago,' he said, and Emma, startled by the boldness of the compliment, raised her fan briefly to cover her face. As if sensing her embarrassment, Mr Henderson began to talk of operas and plays in a light, amusing way. His eyes were admiring, and Emma found it balm to her wounded soul to be flattered by this handsome Englishman instead of being misled and betrayed by a foreign count whose tastes obviously ran to blowsy blondes.

'I have a box at the opera, Lady Wright,' Mr Henderson was now saying. 'Cannot I persuade you and your companion to join me this evening?'

'That is very kind of you, sir,' said Emma gently, 'but, you forget, I am in mourning.'

'Not at all. You would not be expected to attend the ball or supper afterward. It might do you good to sit quietly in the back of my box and listen to the music.'

Emma hesitated. She was about to refuse when she suddenly thought of the comte arriving in the evening and finding her out instead of sitting waiting for him.

'Thank you, Mr Henderson,' she said with a smile. 'I should like that above all things.'

The comte arrived at Emma's house in Curzon Street in low spirits. Madame Beauregard had finally told him the name of the man who had been with her in the Yellow Saloon. She said she had been flirting with a great many men that evening at the Harveys' ball and her husband had been insanely jealous. They had retired together to the Yellow Saloon and had a blazing row, followed by a passionate reconciliation. Lady Harvey had walked in on them, had seen only Madame Beauregard's face, and had assumed the gentleman with her to be a lover. It was all very neat. But somehow, after he asked the all-important question about the Yellow Saloon, Madame Beauregard had ceased to talk radical politics with him and behind her caresses and wooing he sensed a withdrawal.

'My lady in the drawing room?' he asked Tamworthy as the butler relieved him of his cloak.

'No, milord,' said Tamworthy. 'My lady is at the opera.'

'Just like that. With whom did she go?'

'A Mr Henderson.'

The comte's face went blank. Then he said, 'Bring some brandy to the drawing room and I will wait for Lady Wright to return.'

The comte tried to settle in the drawing room, to read, to do anything to pass the time. But every time he heard a carriage in the street, he leapt to his feet and ran to the window only to retire, disappointed. His anger against Emma grew as the time passed. Here he was, giving up his valuable evening on her behalf and she had gone jaunting off to the opera with one of the very men she ought to avoid. Fear for her sharpened his anger, and when she finally returned, the normally sunny-natured comte was in a towering rage.

'How dare you go out without consulting me first?' he raged.

Emma's face went blank, as dead and blank as it used to go when faced with her husband's tantrums. 'A Mr Henderson kindly asked me to share his box at the opera,' she said. 'I am tired of being mewed up here like a prisoner.'

Behind the angry couple, Miss Tippet's stomach gave a faint wailing sound followed by a rumble like thunder. The comte rounded on the companion. 'Miss Tippet, take yourself off and have supper, have twenty suppers, but leave us alone.'

'You are not to be alone with Lady Wright this late at night,' said Miss Tippet, feeling very noble indeed, for she was ravenously hungry.

'You may retire and leave the door open when you go,' snapped the comte. 'Do as you are told, woman!'

Miss Tippet gave a heavy sniff and lumbered from the room.

Emma had never stood up to her husband, but somehow this was different. She could not ever remember being quite so angry. 'How dare you complain about my innocent outing with a perfectly respectable gentleman who was the soul of consideration and courtesy when you, my lord, pass your time with an overblown blonde.'

His face relaxed and his eyes began to sparkle.

'Madame Beauregard,' he said. 'I saw you in the park, but I did not think you had seen me. Madame Beauregard was in the Yellow Saloon at midnight with a man. I had to find out who that man was. She now says it was her husband.'

'I don't believe a word of it,' said Emma crossly. 'You were obviously *doting* on the creature.'

'Do not be silly. I was pretending to dote on her to get information. Madame Beauregard wishes for the restoration of Napoleon.'

'Then report her to the authorities!'

'They would only laugh at me. Did they arrest Byron or any of the others who so loudly cheered Napoleon while England was at war?'

'But there can be no connection,' said Emma. 'My husband celebrated all Wellington's victories. He did not belong to the anti-war faction. What reason could he possibly have for supporting our enemies?'

'Money,' said the comte tersely. 'He loved money. He must have loved money. A respectable Member of Parliament does not risk his reputation by using marked cards unless money is the main love of his life.'

'But Napoleon is imprisoned. He cannot do any harm now!'

'Were he to escape, he could do a great deal of harm. And now we come to your beau of this evening. James Henderson was present at that ball and playing cards with your husband. And now, out of the blue, he decides to pay court to you.'

Emma turned and looked in the glass over the

fireplace. She was wearing an opera gown of dull green brocade. Fine emeralds flashed at her neck and emerald earrings set in old gold hung from her ears. Her thick black hair was dressed high on her head in one of the latest Roman fashions, and one glossy black ringlet gleamed against the whiteness of her shoulder.

'Do you not think, my dear Comte, that he might simply be interested in me for myself alone?' Her voice was as teasing and mocking as the comte's could be when he was carrying on a flirtation.

'In this case, no,' said the comte acidly. 'Stop preening in front of the glass and listen to me . . .'

'I am not preening. Would you not be better pursuing your French doxy instead of insulting me?' demanded Emma, her eyes flashing.

He seized her by the shoulders and looked down into her eyes. And then the anger left his own and he said softly, '*Ma foi*, you are so beautiful.' His hands slid down her arms to her elbows and he pulled her against him. He bent his head toward her mouth.

She began to tremble. Her experiences in the bedchamber with her husband had been highly unpleasant. Scenes crowded into her frightened mind, and she wrenched herself out of his arms.

A footman entered the room, carrying a laden tray, which he set on a low table. Miss Tippet came in and sat down in front of the tray and began to eat steadily.

The comte drew Emma over to the window and said in a low voice, 'I frightened you. What did I do?'

Emma shook her head dumbly and looked at the floor. The comte glanced at the companion. Miss Tippet was raising a large meat pie in both hands to her mouth. The comte put a finger under Emma's chin and tilted her face up, seeing a gleam of tears in her eyes.

'Why! What a brute I am,' he said softly. 'That husband of yours. Were he alive today, I would cheerfully shoot him myself.'

He released her and said gently, 'Come and sit down and tell me what James Henderson said. Did he ask about papers, about your husband's effects?'

'No,' said Emma, feeling almost as shaken by his kindness and intuition as she had been a moment before when she thought he was about to kiss her. 'He hardly mentioned the murder at all except to say he hoped the villain would be caught. He . . . he . . . was very kind, and it was pleasant just to listen to the music.'

'Well, we'll see what happens. But your husband's note said meet H. in the Yellow Saloon, and here we have Henderson. It might be better not to see him again.'

'But I have promised to go driving with him tomorrow,' protested Emma.

'Then I suppose a drive will be safe enough.'

Some imp prompted Emma to say, 'Despite the chaperonage of Miss Tippet, any man interested in marrying me would not like to learn that you spend your nights here.'

'But you said you would never marry again!'

'I've changed my mind,' said Emma in a voice that sounded dreadfully pettish to her own ears.

The comte said something that sounded like *tcha* and strode from the room.

'And there's no sense in females,' he grumbled to Jolly the next day. 'There I am, on hand, to help all I can, and she decides to go and get spoony over Henderson and refuses to suspect him of an ulterior motive.'

'He may not have an ulterior motive,' said Jolly lazily, knocking ash from his cheroot to fall among the oyster shells on the coffee room floor. Both men had gone to the Five Trees coffee house in St James's to discuss the problem of the Wright murder.

'What makes you say that?' demanded the comte.

'I was at the opera last night and saw Lady Wright. She looked more beautiful than ever before. She is also a rich widow. Now that most folk don't think she topped her husband, they'll be queuing at her door to marry her.'

'The deuce!'

'Want her for yourself, dear chap?'

'I simply don't want my investigations complicated,' snapped the comte.

In a coffee house not very far away, Mr Henderson sat with his friends, Lord Framley and Lord Fletcher.

'Paying court to the pretty widow, I hear?' jeered Lord Fletcher.

'Yes,' said James Henderson calmly, 'and not

another word on that subject in that tone of voice or I will have to call you out.'

'A word of caution,' said Lord Framley heavily. 'I think that secretary hanged himself and the Comte Saint-Juste was on hand to tell everyone it was murder because he wants to protect Lady Wright. But just because fickle society has suddenly decided she didn't commit murder doesn't mean she didn't do it.'

'That's enough!' cried James Henderson furiously. 'That comte has wound his way into her life by promising to find the murderer. Well, *I* shall volunteer my services instead. She would be better off with an Englishman than with some posturing mountebank of a French count! There must be something in that house that she has overlooked, some papers, something. Hey, waiter, bring pen and ink and paper! I shall send her a note and ask her to look again. You know what a secretive cove Sir Benjamin was. I bet he hid things under the floorboards or in the walls.'

Early in the afternoon, Emma received a visitor, a Miss Philby. She asked Tamworthy to send the lady up; although she had not heard of her, she assumed her visitor to be a kindly member of society come to call.

Miss Philby was a tall, statuesque brunette, not in the first flush of youth, but with a certain sad dignity.

'Lady Wright,' she said, 'may I speak to you alone?'

'Of course,' said Emma. 'Miss Tippet, if you would be so good . . .'

Miss Tippet sighed and looked at the tray in front of her, which contained a large plate of sandwiches. 'Call the maid and tell her to carry those to the saloon for you,' said Emma, and Miss Tippet visibly brightened, planning to order the maid to bring more food at the same time.

When the companion had ambled out, holding a sandwich in each hand as if afraid to be parted for a moment from food, Emma asked Miss Philby to be seated. 'What do you wish to speak to me about?' she asked.

'I will come straight to the point,' said Miss Philby. She had a very beautiful voice and a fine pair of grey eyes. 'I have been the mistress of Mr James Henderson for some time. It has been understood that we will marry as soon as we find money to pay his gambling debts.'

Emma stared at her visitor, her eyes wide with shock. 'Why should I believe you?' she asked.

'Would you recognize his handwriting?' asked Miss Philby.

'No . . . yes. I had a letter from him earlier today. I have it here.'

'Then read this.' Miss Philby took a letter from her reticule and handed it to Emma. Emma slowly opened it.

'My dearest love,' she read. 'When will you be mine? When will you promise to be with me for the rest of our lives?' The rest of the letter was of such an intimate nature that Emma blushed. But she steeled herself to compare the handwriting and signature with the letter Mr Henderson had sent her. They matched exactly.

'Why are you here?' asked Emma.

'I think you know,' said Miss Philby with quiet dignity. 'You were seen at the opera last night with my James.' Emma winced. 'Please promise me you will never see him again.'

'That is easily done,' said Emma. 'You have my promise.'

Miss Philby rose gracefully to her feet and moved to the door. She paused on the threshold. 'I thank you,' she said, 'and my unborn child thanks you.'

And with that final bombshell, she quietly left the room.

SIX

A week had passed since Emma had learned the shocking news about Mr Henderson, a week during which the comte had turned up at Curzon Street very late at night and had gone almost immediately to bed.

Matilda and Annabelle were once more on calling terms, cards and invitations for Emma were beginning to arrive almost daily, and life appeared to be resuming an air of normality. There was only the comte's nightly visits to remind Emma that the murderer of her husband was still at large.

The fine weather had broken and the days were unseasonably cold. The Harveys had condescended to invite Emma to one of their breakfasts. Lady Harvey felt that if she invited Emma, the comte might attend as well and perhaps show her more of that strangely flattering interest. Lord Harvey, slightly surprised that his wife should wish to include Emma in the party – not because she had been suspected of murder, but because he considered her rank in society to be not quite of the first stare – nonetheless agreed. He found it easier to agree with his more forceful wife on all points.

Emma had not seen Mr Henderson since the time she had refused to go driving with him, and when she arrived was dismayed to find him among the guests. But Mr Henderson's pride had obviously been wounded, for he treated her to a brief chilly nod and then avoided her. The breakfast, which began at three in the afternoon, was served indoors instead of in the garden as had originally been planned. Before the company took their places at the table, Emma found herself surrounded by curious people eager to know if anything else had happened that might throw light on the identity of the murderer. Henderson, Lord Framley and Lord Fletcher were standing together; slightly behind them was Madame Beauregard with a small, sallow man who appeared to be her husband. Emma looked at all the eager faces and gave a little shrug.

'I am afraid I will never find out who killed Sir Benjamin,' she said. Then she saw the comte arriving, and some imp prompted her to say, 'But I am sure there must be documents or papers still in the house, in a secret hiding place, which might give me a clue. After all, whoever killed my husband was someone with whom he entrusted the keys to the back door of the house and his study, someone he did not want either myself or the servants to know about. He was always making notes. I am sure I shall hit on something. I plan to redecorate, and perhaps the joiners and builders can take the place apart before they begin their work–' The comte entered the room and she broke off.

She shivered slightly. It was as if the temperature had suddenly dropped. There was a creeping feeling of menace in the air, and everyone was watching her steadily.

Then the comte came forward to bow before her, impeccable in Weston's tailoring, his cravat a miracle of intricate pleats and folds, a diamond winking at his throat, and a large diamond and sapphire ring on his finger. 'How solemn you all are!' cried the comte. 'Perhaps you *all* murdered Sir Benjamin. But me, I know *why* Sir Benjamin was murdered. He was a French spy.'

There was a shocked silence and then a burst of laughter. The comte was ever original. People began to rise and move through to the dining room to take their places at table, once more a carelessly unheeding group of society figures, snuffboxes snapping open and shut, scented handkerchiefs waving, fans fluttering, and jewels glittering.

'Why did you say that?' demanded Emma in a fierce undertone as the comte escorted her.

'For the same reason as you threw out that statement about getting the joiners and builders to search the house thoroughly. Oh, yes, I heard you. Your voice was loud and clear and reached me as I was handing my cloak to the butler. You, too, want to prompt some action rather than sit and wait like a tethered goat for the tiger to arrive. We are to sit together, you see, so you will now have ample time to tell me why Mr Henderson looks at you so coldly and why you refused to go driving with him. You said you had the headache, but what is the actual truth?'

'It is no matter,' said Emma. She had remained silent not out of loyalty to Mr Henderson, but through concern for the poor and pregnant Miss Philby. Emma, now seated with the comte on her right, noticed Lady Harvey throw a glowing look in the comte's direction, and felt angry and ill at ease. What did she really know of this French comte? He seemed armoured in frivolity and good tailoring. At a separate table for the less distinguished guests, Miss Tippet was sitting, a knife and fork grasped in her pudgy hands and a look of eager anticipation on her face. And yet she had eaten two beefsteaks before leaving the house.

'I am glad I am rich', said Emma, 'otherwise I would find the burden of feeding Miss Tippet too great.'

'Amazing Falstaff of a woman,' murmured the comte, raising his quizzing glass and surveying the companion. 'She will eat herself to death one day. Now, before the gentleman on your other side claims your attention, I must tell you I have procured a box at the playhouse for us for this evening. No, do not protest. It will do us both good. I can see by the shadows under your eyes that you have been sleeping badly and I, too, rouse at every creak and sound during the night. We will enjoy the play – it is a silly melodrama – and then we shall return and sleep and forget about murders.'

'Does Miss Tippet go with us?' asked Emma.

He sighed. 'No, you are a respectable widow and there is no need for her company. She would probably start to eat the box if kept away from the kitchen too long.'

The gentleman on Emma's other side turned out to be Lord Framley. He asked her whether she was enjoying the Season, and when she said quietly, as much as could be expected, he leered at her and said she didn't seem to be mourning her husband much. His pale eyes raked over her gown of lavender muslin edged with grey ribbon in a way that made Emma wish the gown were thicker and not cut so low at the neck. The lady on the comte's other side was Madame Beauregard, and to Emma's intense annoyance, the comte seemed determined to talk to her for the rest of the meal. Emma found that Lord Framley was actually making an effort to flirt with her and could only be glad when at last the long meal was over. On the one side, Lord Framley with his nudges and leers and innuendos was making her uncomfortable, and on her other side, the sheer physical presence of the comte was doing odd things to her body. She was acutely aware of him, of the hidden strength of the arm in the well-tailored sleeve, of the strong legs under the table, of the slim waist, and the long-fingered hands that had grasped her so tightly that time he had seemed about to kiss her.

She wished Annabelle and Matilda were present and then, in the next moment, was glad they were not. She sensed that they did not approve of the comte and were secretly shocked at his nightly visits.

And what would happen to her when the murderer was found, or when the comte tired of the chase? Before his arrival, she would have thought that to be free of Sir Benjamin, and free to enjoy the company of her two friends, was all that she could possibly hope for. She would not admit to any strong feelings for the comte and would tell herself only that he was an unsettling and irritating man. Apart from the fact that well-bred ladies were not supposed to think about intimacies, Sir Benjamin's bedroom antics had effectively put paid to any temptation that Emma might have had to indulge in daydreams of love-making.

The comte was now promenading in the chilly garden with Madame Beauregard, who appeared not to feel the cold despite the fact she was wearing damped muslin. Emma found Lord Framley again at her elbow, this time asking her if she would go for a drive with him on the following day. She mendaciously said she was not free and moved away quickly toward Miss Tippet, wishing as she did so that the lady were more companion and less human pig.

Emma had been determined to tell the comte she could not accept his invitation to the playhouse, but when she sat down beside Miss Tippet and saw the crumbs on Miss Tippet's bosom and the chewed chicken wing nestling on top of Miss Tippet's cameo brooch, she decided to go after all and get at least one evening away from her dreadful companion. She told Miss Tippet of the proposed visit to the playhouse and Miss Tippet began to show alarming signs of taking her duties seriously. 'For it is not proper,' said Miss Tippet severely. 'People will *talk*.'

'Society has already said a great many evil things about me,' snapped Emma. 'A few more won't matter.'

'I suppose you'll be safe enough,' sniffed Miss Tippet. 'He obviously dotes on that Frenchie woman. Did you ever see such a gown? And not even a handkerchief in her garter.' Miss Tippet breathed heavily through her nose with the irritating wheeze of the overfed. 'Oh, here's m'cousin.'

Jolly wandered amiably over, sat down next to them, and introduced himself to Emma. 'I was just telling Lady Wright,' said Miss Tippet, 'that the Comte Saint-Juste is making a cake of himself over that Frenchwoman. And her here with her husband, too! But, then, your friends never had any morals.'

'He's investigating Sir Benjamin's murder,' said Jolly, throwing Emma a comical look of dismay.

'So that's what it's called,' said Miss Tippet with a breathy laugh. 'In my day it was called–'

'Never mind what they said in your day,' interrupted Jolly hastily. 'Care to walk with me for a little, Lady Wright?'

Emma rose and went off on his arm, grateful for his undemanding company. It was a formal, regimented garden, still laid out in the Elizabethan manner with clipped yew hedges and flower beds edged with lavender. The smell of the yew reminded Emma of churchyards and funerals. They passed the comte and Madame Beauregard. The comte smiled and bowed; Madame Beauregard looked briefly at Emma, a small curved smile on her mouth and a hard look of hate in her eyes.

'By George!' exclaimed Jolly as they moved on, 'That Frenchwoman looks jealous of you.'

'She has no reason,' said Emma quietly.

'Oh, I don't know,' said Jolly, glancing down at her. 'Never known Saint-Juste to take such an interest in anything before.'

'It's the joy of the chase,' said Emma with a bleak little laugh. 'A fox, perhaps, would do just as well.'

'Oh, he don't hunt,' said Jolly cheerfully. 'Can't stand it.'

'He considers it cruel?'

'Perhaps, but he says he don't like his clothes getting muddy.'

'I should have guessed,' said Emma in a thin voice. 'My lord does not take anything seriously.'

'Never had reason before to take anything seriously,' said Jolly. 'His grandparents actually supported the revolution in France . . . well, before it got under way. But they got topped just like the others. I think that's a serious enough thing for a whole lifetime.'

'How dreadful!' Emma raised her hands to her cheeks.

'They're a cruel race, the French,' said Jolly easily, forgetting he was also talking about his best friend. 'Cut your throat as soon as look at you.'

Again, Emma had that odd feeling she did not know the comte at all. She had half a mind to refuse his invitation to the play, but that would mean spending an evening watching Miss Tippet eat. The Harveys' breakfast was to be followed by a dance, but because of her mourning state, Emma could not dance. At least the play would take her mind off her troubles.

But at the playhouse, her treacherous body seemed constantly aware of the comte, of every shift of muscle, of the curve of his mouth, of his ridiculously long lashes, of the faint scent of cologne that he wore.

The play was silly. It was called *The Wicked Squire* and followed the well-worn theme of the heroine and her aged mother being put out in the snow if the heroine did not marry the squire. And then Emma sat up straight and leaned forward. There was something familiar about the heroine's voice. Her name on the bills had proclaimed her to be a Mrs Jessica Friendly. Emma fumbled in her reticule and took out a small pair of opera glasses, studied the stage, and then let them drop into her lap with a gasp. For

Mrs Friendly was none other than Mr Henderson's Miss Philby.

'What is wrong?' asked the comte sharply.

'I have been the victim of a cruel trick,' said Emma slowly. 'I did not tell you because I thought I was protecting a good lady's name. The reason I did not go driving with Mr Henderson was a Miss Philby called on me and said that she was not only Mr Henderson's mistress but also the mother of his child. Why would anyone do such a thing?'

'Obviously to stop you getting close to Mr Henderson,' said the comte. 'But why? Did Henderson say anything about the murder?'

'He sent me a letter saying he wished to help to solve the murder and that he was sure Sir Benjamin must have papers hidden in the house.'

'And so someone hired an actress to put you off! We'll go and visit her afterward and see what we can find out.'

But when they met Mrs Friendly in the Green Room after the performance, she looked boldly at Emma and disclaimed all knowledge of her and of a Mr Henderson, and would not be shaken.

'Someone is paying her well,' muttered the comte as he helped Emma into his carriage.

'But there is more!' exclaimed Emma. 'She showed me a love letter from Mr Henderson, and I compared it with the letter he had sent me earlier, a letter in which he suggested there might yet be papers hidden in the house, and handwriting and signature both matched.'

'Gentlemen are always sending passionate love letters to actresses,' said the comte. 'I have done so myself. He could have sent her one some time ago. I had better see Henderson tomorrow and find out who knew of his proposed drive with you and who knew he had sent you a letter suggesting you tear the house apart.'

But that remark of the comte's that he, too, had sent passionate letters to actresses had sent Emma's spirits plummeting to a new low. There was no sign of Miss Tippet, and Emma only sat briefly with the comte in the drawing room over the tea tray before pleading tiredness and retiring to bed.

She slept badly, tossing and turning, plagued with dreams of the comte making love to Madame Beauregard. She awoke with a start, and by the light of the bed lamp looked at the clock. Two in the morning. She turned over on her side and tried to get to sleep again.

And then she heard a furtive, intermittent tapping sound through the stillness of the sleeping house. She rose and pulled a thin muslin wrapper over her nightgown, picked up a candle and lit it, and cautiously opened the bedroom door.

Silence.

And then just as she was turning away that tap-tap-tapping started up again.

She crept toward the landing, the long skirts of her nightgown making a whispering noise on the floor. She leaned over the banister. The tapping was coming from the ground floor. She made her way cautiously down to the next landing and again leaned over.

The study door was open and a yellow shaft of light from the oil lamp that stood on a table inside the study shone out into the hall.

She inched her way down the stairs, blowing out the candle as she did so. She would try to get a glimpse of whoever it was in the study and then rouse the servants.

She reached the open door of the study, set the candlestick down on a side table, and looked inside.

The Comte Saint-Juste, attired in a garishly embroidered dressing gown, was tapping at the panelled walls of the study. She was about to call him when she suddenly felt a frisson of fear. Why was he so assiduously searching in the middle of the night when he could easily search with the help of the servants in broad daylight? His profile was toward her and his face looked grim and set.

And then he suddenly turned, as if aware of her gaze, and looked straight at her, his eyes quite blank. Then he smiled, and his face was restored to its usual, charming, smiling . . . mask?

'What are you doing?' asked Emma, her own voice sounding oddly faint to her ears.

'Looking for more evidence,' he said lightly.

'Why now?' demanded Emma. 'You have all the time in the world to search during daylight hours.'

'I could not sleep,' he said. 'I was thinking of you.'

He walked toward her, and Emma backed away into the darkness of the hall, all at once aware of the thinness of her nightdress covered only with a frilly muslin wrapper.

'I suggest you leave your investigation until morning,' said Emma, 'and get the servants to help you.'

'As you will. You look so very beautiful. Your hair is like a midnight river.'

'Stay away from me!' said Emma.

He stopped and looked at her, his eyes searching hers in the darkness. 'All men are not as your husband was,' he said softly. 'I could show you . . .'

He moved quickly and caught her in his arms. She stood rigid with fright.

His head bent down toward her mouth and she closed her eyes. His mouth would crush hers and his teeth would grate against her own. His hand would squeeze and crush and maul her breast – such was Emma's experience of love-making. But the mouth that met her own was gentle and warm and caressing, the body, now pressed tightly against hers, firm and muscled under the dressing gown. The kiss grew deeper and more searching. She felt a hot yearning, and then her body went on fire and fused into his own. Her hands rose to caress the crisp fair curls at his neck. He freed his mouth and looked down into her eyes. 'You enchant me,' he said huskily.

A voice of reason screamed in Emma's head. *He is a practiced seducer. He has not said one word of love.* She wrenched her treacherous, betraying body out of his arms and ran up the stairs, not stopping until she reached the sanctuary of her room.

She locked the door and then leaned against it,

shaking. He could no longer stay in her house. She might find the courage in the morning to tell him to leave. She was ashamed of her own aching body. Her breasts felt heavy and swollen, and there was a pain at the pit of her stomach. He had bewitched her as he had bewitched so many women. The murder must be forgotten. Better to live at risk without the comte's help than to lose her soul to an uncaring fribble.

She fell asleep at last, rehearsing dismissal speeches in her head, as yet unaware that tragedy would step in to make any such speeches unnecessary.

Austin was brushing out Emma's hair in the morning when she said, 'Did you get your present, my lady?'

'No,' said Emma, regarding the maid in the mirror. 'What present?'

'It was the most gigantic box of sugar plums you ever did see. Came while you were at the play.'

'From whom?'

'Don't know, my lady. Just a card to say that they was from an admirer. Tamworthy took them up to the drawing room and Miss Tippet said she would see that you got them.'

Despite her worry about the comte, Emma began to laugh. 'Poor Miss Tippet. It must have been more than flesh and blood could bear. She has probably eaten the lot and is now wondering what to tell me.' Then Emma frowned. She wanted Miss Tippet to be present when she told the comte that he must no longer spend his nights in her home. Then he could smile and charm for all his might, but Miss Tippet would be protection.

'I can finish dressing myself, Austin,' she said. 'Go and rouse Miss Tippet and tell her I wish her to attend me.'

'Very good, my lady.'

Austin left and Emma sighed. What a good maid she was! And how good and loyal the other servants were. If only this awful menace would go away and leave her free to lead a normal life.

And then a piercing scream seemed to rend the house from top to bottom.

Emma ran from her room, half dressed, toward the direction of those terrible screams. They were coming from Miss Tippet's bedchamber. She collided with the comte, who came darting out of his room. 'Something awful has happened,' gasped Emma. He pushed past her, his face looking harder and older. Followed by the servants and Emma, he strode into Miss Tippet's bedroom. Austin was standing by the bed. Her screams had stopped and she was sobbing hysterically. Miss Tippet lay half in and half out of the bed, her face purple, her eyes staring, her tongue sticking out. Sugar plums lay strewn across the bedspread, and a large box lay upended on the floor where it had fallen.

'Silence!' ordered the comte, thrusting the shaking, weeping maid toward Emma. He stooped over Miss Tippet and then straightened up. 'Call the runners,' he said over his shoulder to Tamworthy.

'But surely she has simply eaten herself to death

and had an apoplexy!' said Emma over the weeping maid's shoulder.

'No, my lady,' said the comte. 'Unless I am very much mistaken, the unfortunate Miss Tippet has been poisoned!'

The rest of the day was a nightmare of comings and goings, of interviews by the authorities, of a visit from a distressed Jolly and his relatives, and of the awful awareness for Emma that the poisoned sugar plums had been meant for herself.

By late afternoon she was looking so white and strained that the comte said urgently, 'Go! Get away from this house. Go and call on one of your friends, the Duchess of Hadshire, say. Take Austin. I will handle any more inquiries.'

'Yes, yes,' agreed Emma in a distracted way. She wished he had not kissed her. Then she might have been able to stay with him and talk away some of her fears. And what if he himself were the murderer? She called for her carriage and departed for Matilda's home, glad to escape.

The duchess was at home, and to Emma's delight was entertaining Annabelle. Both women listened in shocked alarm as Emma told them of the latest developments.

'You must not return,' said Matilda firmly. 'You must stay here with me. Your maid may return with my servants and collect your baggage.' She reached out a hand to ring the bell, but, at that moment, the double doors to the duchess's charming Rose

Saloon were thrown open by two liveried footmen, and the Duke of Hadshire walked in.

Matilda's hand dropped from the bell as she rose to face her husband, who had taken out his quizzing glass and was surveying Emma as if she were a new and curious type of beetle.

'It is all most shocking, my love,' said Matilda. 'Poor Lady Wright's companion has been murdered . . . poisoned . . . and by a box of sugar plums intended for her. She must not return there, and so I have asked her to stay with us for a little. Our servants can collect her trunks and . . .'

Her voice trailed away before her husband's raised eyebrows and frosty stare.

'More mayhem?' he asked in his thin, precise voice. 'I am sorry, Lady Wright, but we cannot allow you to reside with us. Your very presence would put our own lives at risk, as someone appears very determined to be rid of you. Not,' he went on, giving Emma a slight bow, 'that we would not normally be charmed, nay, delighted to have your fair presence in our household.'

Matilda's little hands tightened into fists. 'A word with you in private,' she said to her husband.

'La! We have no secrets and therefore anything we say is for public ears. Rougemont!' he called over his shoulder. His valet came quietly in and stood to attention. 'Rougemont, Lady Wright and Mrs Carruthers were just on their way out. I am sure you will be charmed to assist them to the door. Ladies, your servant.'

The air of veiled menace in the duke's manner and the brutish air of his servant were enough for Annabelle and Emma, who quickly took their leave. Outside on the pavement, Annabelle said tearfully, 'Oh, if only you could return with me, but Mr Carruthers is hardly ever sober and he . . . he can be quite violent, especially when he has lost as much at the tables as he has done recently.'

Emma returned home, her heart sinking as Curzon Street approached. The London streets were quiet. Society was all indoors, preparing for the evening's entertainments that lay ahead. A lamplighter was climbing up his ladder to light the parish lamp at the entrance to Shepherd Market. Emma could smell the whale oil from his can as she passed and the smell of meat from the now-closed butchers' shops in the market.

She felt very alone in the world and then chided herself for forgetting that she had Austin and the other servants. But it was hard to forgive her parents for not rushing to her side. She had written to them an express about the murder of the secretary but had received no reply at all. There was only the comte left, a man who devastated her senses so that she could not think about him clearly.

And yet when she entered the house and was told that the comte had removed his belongings, she felt a sense of loss and a deeper sense of isolation. But how could he stay? She was without a chaperone. Miss Tippet's relatives had removed her body after it had been examined by two physicians and a pathologist, said Tamworthy in a hushed voice. Miss Tippet had indeed been poisoned. If Tamworthy might make a humble suggestion? My lady would be better to remove to the country on the morrow, away from this evil place.

'Of course you are right,' said Emma. 'And yet to run like a coward! There must be something in this house, Tamworthy, that the murderer or murderers know of and fear. Tomorrow morning, send for joiners and builders and carpenters, and we will take this place apart piece by piece, floorboard by floorboard, and *then* we will leave for the country.'

But Emma did not feel nearly so brave when she sat alone in the drawing room over the tea tray. She had a mad impulse to ring for all the servants and ask them to join her. But that impulse quickly died. Servants were even more rigidly aware of the caste system than their betters. They would stand politely to attention and she would be made to feel even more uneasy than she did with her own company. A footman came in and made up the fire and lit the lamps and the candelabrum.

Emma tried to read, and then she crossed to the piano and began to play softly. If only the comte would come so that she might tell him how she distrusted him. What was he doing?

In the servants' hall, Tamworthy was telling the others about the proposed move to the country, 'although my lady plans to have this place ripped apart before she leaves.' Mrs Chumley, the housekeeper, exclaimed in dismay. There would be plaster dust everywhere.

The little housemaid, Bertha, put her hand to her brow. 'I feel ever so faint,' she whimpered. 'Couldn't I just step up the stairs to the street for a breath of fresh air?'

'You are always going up to the street,' said Mrs Chumley sharply. 'I think you have a caller.'

'Oh, no,' said Bertha. 'Which of them grand London servants would come calling on a country maid?'

'Very well,' said Mrs Chumley, 'but only for a moment.'

Bertha scuttled off. Soon she was standing at the top of the area steps, straining her eyes into the blackness of the night. There was a lamp in its hooped bracket over the main door, but it left the top of the area steps in shadow.

Suddenly she saw a cloaked figure moving toward her and bobbed a curtsy. 'Well,' said the man who approached her. 'What news?'

'I should get into ever so much trouble if I was found out,' whispered Bertha.

'I told you, I am in love with your mistress and her welfare is my sole concern,' said the man. 'Out with it.' He held out a crown piece which glittered faintly in the darkness.

Bertha pocketed the coin. 'My lady leaves for the country tomorrow.'

'Good, she will be safe there.'

'But afore she goes, she's got joiners and builders coming to rip the house apart.'

'Why?' The man's voice was sharp with alarm.

'Well, Mr Tamworthy, that's our butler, he do say that Sir Benjamin was a great one for taking notes and that my lady thinks there might be papers hidden behind the walls or panelling, for there waren't nothing in his study.'

Down below, the kitchen door creaked and then Mrs Chumley's voice could be heard calling, 'Are you there, Bertha?'

Bertha let out a startled squeak and scurried down the stairs.

The man drew his cloak around him and hurried off down the street.

SEVEN

The comte went to call on Lady Harvey. He was all at once sure that the man in the Yellow Saloon with Madame Beauregard had not been her husband. He hoped Lord Harvey would be absent, but suddenly felt he could not wait any longer to question Lady Harvey, and he was determined to question her whether her husband was there or not.

He was lucky. To his polite inquiry, the Harveys' butler said that Lord Harvey was at White's and Lady Harvey was in her boudoir. Lady Harvey was delighted to receive the comte. She had thought and dreamed of him constantly, although, being a sensible woman, had no thought of setting up an affair. She merely wanted to hang on to the dream that this desirable Frenchman found her attractive.

But when he put the all-important question to her,

she pouted and turned away. 'So you are still interested in Lady Wright?' she said.

'Madame,' said the comte with his hand over his heart, 'I am merely trying to track down a murderer. I beg your help.'

Lady Harvey frowned. Had not the guilty gentleman himself called on her to beg her secrecy? She had no intention of betraying him. There was no longer anything of the lover about the comte. She was sadly disappointed in him.

'Madame Beauregard,' pursued the comte, too worried about Emma to play the lover, 'tells me that the gentleman was her husband.'

'Well, there you have it,' said Lady Harvey lightly. 'I am sure you believe every word she says.'

'My lady, I am certain that man was someone else, and you know very well who it was.'

'If you choose to doubt my word,' said Lady Harvey, becoming angry, 'then you may take your leave!'

In vain did the comte persist in trying to make her tell the truth. Piqued at his lack of interest in her and his obviously overwhelming concern for the welfare of Lady Wright, Lady Harvey grew petulant and sulky and he was forced to bow his way out without having found anything.

He next tracked down Mr Henderson and told that horrified man of Mrs Friendly's masquerade as his supposed mistress.

'The deuce!' cried Mr Henderson. 'Yes, I did write her a letter. You know how one does; it means nothing. She must have kept it. Who paid her to perform such a trick?'

'I have an idea. You sent Lady Wright a letter suggesting she tear the house apart, and shortly after that your supposed mistress visited her. Who knew you were going to tell Lady Wright to look for papers?'

Mr Henderson looked bewildered and then his face cleared. 'No one sinister. Only Framley and Fletcher.'

'Where are they this evening?'

'Blessed if I know,' said Mr Henderson. 'I say, you don't suspect one of them. I mean, they haven't the brains or the energy.'

'*Someone* murdered not only Sir Benjamin, but also the secretary and the companion,' said the comte.

'What companion?' asked Mr Henderson, his eyes wide. 'You mean that fat woman?'

'Yes, I mean that fat woman. Someone really meant to murder Lady Wright by sending her a box of poisoned sugar plums, which that poor and greedy companion ate. I mean to find those two gentlemen this evening!'

But search as he might, the comte could find neither Framley nor Fletcher.

Annabelle, Mrs Carruthers, was sitting hemming handkerchiefs in her small drawing room when she heard her husband's footsteps on the stairs. She jabbed the needle nervously into her finger and looked apprehensively toward the door. Would he be drunk again? How on earth were they going to manage for money?

The door swung open and Mr Guy Carruthers stood on the threshold, a huge bouquet of hot-house flowers in one hand and a box of cakes in the other. His once-handsome face was smiling, and to Annabelle's great relief he looked relatively sober.

He came forward and kissed her on the cheek, dropped the flowers in her lap, and placed the box of cakes on her work table.

'Great news, my sweeting,' he said, sinking down in a chair opposite her and stretching out his long legs. 'All out debts are settled and we have money to spare.'

'Oh, Guy,' said Annabelle, beginning to cry with relief. 'I have been so worried.'

'There now, puss. I am a wicked brute and a bad husband. Hey, I'll tell you what you must do. That friend of yours, Lady Wright, having a bad time, ain't she? Well, now we can afford to put her up. Get her to stay with you.'

'Guy, Guy, that would be wonderful.'

'Knew you'd like the idea,' he said with a grin. 'Tell you what I did. Took the liberty of sending that lazy page of ours off with a note inviting her. Told her to come early. Come at nine in the morning and no later, that's what I said.'

'Oh, you nincompoop. That's much too early for London!' cried Annabelle. 'But no matter. I shall tell the maid to make up the bed in the spare room, that is if we still have a maid.'

'You still have your Alice. Told her I'd pay her and that boy in the morning. Now, what about a celebration? Play something for me. It's an age since we had a domestic evening.'

Annabelle felt for the first time that she could begin to learn to love this maddening husband of hers. As her fingers rippled over the keys, she made a vow that she would do everything in her power to make this marriage work, forgetting in her new-found hope and happiness that she had made that same vow so many times before.

Emma was delighted with the invitation and saw nothing odd in being asked to present herself at Annabelle's at nine in the morning. Before she went to bed, she summoned Tamworthy and told him that she would be going to Mrs Carruthers's home for a short visit and to make sure he supervised the work of the builders and watch that they did not make too much mess and to report to her if anything was found.

She was relieved to be leaving. Miss Tippet's fat ghost seemed to haunt every corner. Menace lurked in every shadow, and she awoke several times during the night, thinking she heard strange noises in the house.

Mr Carruthers had asked her not to bring her maid, as they did not have enough room for Austin.

'Don't seem right you going without me,' said Austin as she dressed her mistress's hair the following morning. 'Never heard the likes before.

They could have put a cot for me in their servants' room.'

'I think, Austin, that perhaps they are more worried about another mouth to feed than finding room for you,' said Emma. 'Do not look so sour. I shall have a splendid time with Mrs Carruthers.' A shadow crossed her face as she thought of Annabelle's erratic husband. But surely he would, as usual, be mostly absent, and, after all, he could not object to her presence as he had invited her himself.

She paid particular attention to her appearance, adjusting a smart new bonnet on her black curls and putting a faint dusting of rouge on her pale cheeks. Her eyes looked enormous in her face. The strain of the murders had made her lose weight and had given her features a fine-drawn look.

She was on the point of leaving, standing in the hall, drawing on her gloves, when Tamworthy answered a knock at the door. A footman in plain livery stood on the step. 'Mr Carruthers's compliments,' he said. 'His carriage is ready and waiting for Lady Wright.'

'My lady has her own carriage,' began Tamworthy but was interrupted by Emma. 'It is all right, Tamworthy,' she said. 'I will take Mr Carruthers's carriage. It is most thoughtful of him.'

The footman walked to the carriage door, opened it, and let down the steps. Emma climbed in, the door was slammed behind her, and the carriage moved off through the quiet London streets.

Emma was looking forward to seeing Annabelle

immensely. She longed to talk about the comte and to resolve her fears and doubts about him.

The carriage came to a halt. Emma looked out of the window, startled. They were not in the street where Annabelle lived, but on the edge of Berkeley Square. And then the carriage door was jerked open and Lord Fletcher climbed inside.

'What is the meaning of this, my lord?' cried Emma as he sat down beside her after shutting the carriage door and rapping on the roof with his cane as a signal for the coachman to move on.

He smiled at her and slowly drew a pistol from his pocket. 'I am too fatigued to give you any explanations,' he said. 'Be quiet and no harm will come to you.'

'It was you all the time,' whispered Emma. 'You killed Sir Benjamin.'

'I said *be quiet*,' he snapped.

Now Lord Fletcher no longer looked like an effeminate fribble. His face wore its customary mask of blanc, but his eyes were as hard as stone.

Emma turned her head away and her hand cautiously reached for the leather strap on the door. If she could jerk down the glass and cry for help . . .

'Hands on your lap. Both of them. Where I can see them,' said Lord Fletcher.

How quiet the streets of London were at this time of day, thought Emma miserably. Would he really shoot her if she made a bid for freedom? She glanced at his set face and repressed a shudder. That look in his eyes said that he would shoot her dead without a second's thought as clearly as if he had spoken.

She sent up a prayer for safety and then her mind began to race. How had Lord Fletcher known about her visit to Annabelle's? Was Annabelle part of the plot? Surely not. But Annabelle's husband was another matter . . .

The carriage lurched to a halt and Emma, glancing out the window, recognized the sedate surroundings of Manchester Square. So she was not to be taken out to some secluded building in the country.

'Now, my lady,' said Lord Fletcher. 'I am going to put this gun in my pocket. You will alight from the carriage and go up the steps. You will not make one move to escape or I shall shoot you through the pocket of my coat and then swear blind it was done by a passing ruffian. See, there is no one about. Do as you are told . . . exactly as you are told.'

Emma got down from the carriage. She looked up appealingly into the footman's face, but he turned his eyes away from her. Conscious every step of the way of Lord Fletcher walking behind her, Emma went up the stone steps. The door of the house opened and a butler said, 'Good morning my lady . . . my lord,' just as if they were making a formal call.

'He is going to shoot me,' whispered Emma desperately, but the butler said, as if she had not spoken, 'Be so good as to step this way.' He flung open the double doors leading to a saloon on the ground floor. Numb with fright, Emma walked inside and let out a small gasp as Madame Beauregard rose to meet her.

'I see you've delivered the package,' said Madame Beauregard to Lord Fletcher over Emma's head. 'Put her in that straight-backed chair over by the fire. Groumand, tie her up.'

'Very good, madam,' said the butler as if replying to a request to serve tea. He put a heavy hand on Emma's shoulder and urged her forward to the chair Madame Beauregard had indicated. He snapped his fingers as Emma shakily sat down and a footman entered bearing lengths of rope. The butler stood to one side while the footman bound Emma's wrists behind her and then bound her ankles.

'Gag her,' said Madame Beauregard. 'I do not want to listen to her. Go and find that little spy of yours, my lord, and we will await events.'

Bertha, the little housemaid, tried to rush through her work. The fine gentleman had said he would pay her handsomely for her help. Letters he had written to a lady of royal birth were hidden somewhere in the house. If they were found, then Bertha was to tie a handkerchief to the railings outside. But how could she, Bertha, find out anything, confined as she was to the upstairs bedrooms by Mrs Chumley?

She hurriedly made Emma's bed after having dusted the room and cleared out the fireplace. She was about to leave and rush downstairs toward where the workmen were tearing down the panelling in the study, when Mrs Chumley appeared in the doorway, barring her way. 'Not so fast, Bertha,' said the housekeeper severely. 'You have been skimping your work of late.'

The housekeeper went to the bed and jerked back the blankets. 'Why, the linen has not been changed and what there is is all crumpled!' Bertha suppressed a groan. 'Do your job properly, or I shall have to speak to Mr Tamworthy about you,' said Mrs Chumley, her lips compressed in a disapproving line. 'Come with me to the linen cupboard and I will give you fresh sheets.'

Just then a footman popped his head round the door. 'That comte's arrived,' he said excitedly, 'and the workmen say they've found something.'

Mrs Chumley gave an exclamation and hurried off. Heart beating hard, Bertha drew a white handkerchief from the pocket of her print dress, waited a few moments, and then slid out of the room and hurried down the stairs. Lord Fletcher watched as the little housemaid appeared at the top of the area steps and began to tie the handkerchief onto the railings. He patted the pocket in which he kept his pistol, and, calling to his coachman to wait, he climbed down from the carriage.

The comte was sitting in the late Sir Benjamin's study. Shattered panelling lay all around him, and plaster dust floated in the shafts of sunlight that streamed in through the windows.

He had asked the workmen to retire while he studied his find. In his hands he held a thick leather-bound book locked with a brass clasp. It had been found in a cupboard in the wall which had been cleverly concealed by a secret door. He took out his penknife, broke the lock on the clasp, and opened the book.

On the first page Sir Benjamin had written: *This is my record of those who have worked with me for the escape and restoration of Napoleon. If I am caught, then it is only right that they should hang with me.*

'Mad logic,' murmured the comte, and read on.

I have no interest in betraying my country, Sir Benjamin had written. Then followed a long essay justifying his traitorous actions, which contained long sections from Thomas Paine's *Rights of Man.* After several pages Sir Benjamin got to the point. He had been recruited by Madame Beauregard and her husband and paid large sums of money to pass on to them information on how well Napoleon was guarded and the names of possible sympathizers in the British government and aristocracy. Sir Benjamin was also to arrange permission for a trip to St Helena, and there he was to seek audience with Napoleon and report back ways and means whereby arms and money might be smuggled to the fallen emperor. The reason for his fortune became obvious. The sums already paid to him had been vast.

'If he is going to reveal names, where are they?' asked the comte aloud, impatiently flicking over the pages. 'Ah, here they are.'

He read, 'We all have code names. I am Corbeau, Madame Beauregard is Rossignol and Lord Fletcher is Hirondelle.' The comte put down the book. *Hirondelle,* he thought. *Fletcher's name. So that was the H. with Madame Beauregard in the Yellow Saloon. They were both there to meet Sir Benjamin. Were they playing at lovers in case anyone entered, or were they really lovers? And did Lady Harvey's entrance spoil the meeting? But nothing matters except that these traitors be caught and my poor Emma's name completely cleared.*

He had been told that Emma had left early to visit the Carrutherses. He rose to his feet. He would go to her immediately and together they would take this book to the authorities.

And then the door opened and Tamworthy announced, 'Lord Fletcher to see you, my lord.'

The comte opened his mouth to call to Tamworthy to summon the servants and seize the traitor, and then his sharp eyes noticed the way Lord Fletcher had his hand thrust in his pocket and the unmistakable shape of a pistol. His thoughts moved like lightning. No doubt Fletcher had killed Sir Benjamin, the secretary and Miss Tippet. He would not hesitate to murder the comte and Emma's servants.

'Leave us,' said the comte to the butler, and then, when Tamworthy had left, he said, 'What brings you here, Fletcher?'

'I will not waste time,' said Lord Fletcher. He drew the pistol from his pocket. 'You have found something.'

The comte noticed bleakly that it was a statement, not a question. So much for Emma's 'loyal' servants.

'You will give it to me now and you will not tell anyone what you have found,' went on Lord Fletcher.

'Do not speak such fustian,' said the comte lightly. 'You cannot shoot me and get away with it, *mon ami.* Not in a house full of servants and builders.'

'No, you are right,' said Lord Fletcher amiably. He put the pistol in his pocket. 'I hold a much more powerful weapon.'

Nothing of the sudden dread he felt showed on the comte's face. 'And what is that?' he asked.

'Lady Wright. Yes, we have her. She is still alive, but one move on your part and we will kill her . . . slowly.'

'I have no love for that thug, bully and maniac, Napoleon,' said the comte. 'I have great love, however, for this adopted country of mine. What is to stop me sacrificing Lady Wright to the higher cause?'

'Your own life, you fool,' said Lord Fletcher, 'and the life of any servant who stands between me and escape. Give me what you have found and do not try to bluff.'

'What makes you think the builders and servants do not know your secret?' asked the comte.

'They have not had time. Besides, they would already have tried to take me prisoner. I would shoot you now and be done with it, for you are a menace with your interfering ways, but I feel sure you will do nothing to put Lady Wright's life in jeopardy. Now, hand it over!'

I must play for time, thought the comte bleakly.

He slowly handed over the book, hoping that Lord Fletcher might study it there and then so that he would have a chance to overpower him, but Lord Fletcher merely smiled thinly and put the book in his pocket.

He backed toward the door. 'Not a word,' he spat out, 'or we will send Lady Wright back to you in pieces.'

When he had left, the comte buried his head in his hands. He could alert the forces of law and order and have them storm Madame Beauregard's house, which is where he was sure Emma was being held. But he was sure Fletcher would kill Emma before she could be reached. For all he knew, she might already be dead.

Why had he not armed himself? All he had in his pocket was a bottle of French perfume he had bought for Emma. He drew it out and looked at it. It was in a green bottle that winked and flashed in its crystal container when he held it up.

He looked at it thoughtfully and then he slowly put it back into his pocket. There was one weapon he could use . . .

'I do not think his affections are deeply engaged,' said Lord Fletcher. He was lounging in a chair in Madame Beauregard's saloon. Emma was still tied to the chair. She was feeling exhausted with fear and emotion. She had been allowed to move only once, and that was to go to the privy in the garden under guard. She had been momentarily relieved that her captors had at least spared her the indignity of soiling herself, but they had promptly regagged and rebound her and had shown no signs of giving her anything to eat. But she roused slightly at the sound of 'he', guessing accurately that they spoke of the comte.

'I pray you,' went on Lord Fletcher earnestly, all foppish mannerisms gone, 'to consider that this fool of a comte may go straight to the authorities.'

Madame Beauregard swung one slippered foot and yawned. 'And if they do? What proof have they? At the first sign of any attack, we get rid of her, protest our innocence, and make our escape. Keep a cool head. It is not an Englishman accusing us but some dilettante comte whom nobody has ever taken seriously.'

'I must remind you that the Comte Saint-Juste has powerful friends. What does Beauregard say?'

'My husband does as he is told. It takes time to make arrangements. This evening or tomorrow, the comte will meet with a sad accident. Then we will dispose of her. Then we will leave for France until all chance of suspicion falling on us has died down.'

'But we have involved so many people. There is that actress . . .'

'Pooh! She thought she was doing it as a joke.'

'Then there is that large friend of Saint-Juste's with the ridiculous nickname . . . Jolly. He will surely step in to help. And what about the housemaid I bribed to get us information? We can't kill them all.'

'I tell you, my friend, we will be safely out of the

country soon, and our spies will tell us whether we can return or not.'

'It is madness to wait.'

'Look out the window. All is quiet. It is my belief that the frivolous comte will shrug off this matter and go back to his idle life. But you fatigue me with your fears. Go out to your oh-so-English clubs and listen. Believe me, you will not hear a murmur, and it will put your mind at rest.'

'I will do that,' said Lord Fletcher edgily. 'I cannot sit here like a rat in a trap.'

Emma watched him go. Madame Beauregard picked up a fashion magazine and began to read an article as if Emma were already dead. Emma feared the Frenchwoman. There was a mad callousness about her. But had she judged the comte accurately? Would he decide, as Madame Beauregard had said, that it was all too much trouble? Perhaps the comte himself was a follower of Napoleon?

Emma closed her eyes, seeing pictures from her life flashing in front of her eyes, her husband's brutal face, his body lying sprawled on the office floor, the comte, laughing and charming and teasing, the feel of his lips against hers, and tears squeezed between her eyelids and rolled down her cheeks.

She would never see him again, never know whether he missed her or not. Or perhaps even now he might be dead.

She heard through her misery a knock at the street door. Then the butler opened the door and said in accents of extreme surprise, 'The Comte

Saint-Juste, madam. Shall I tell him there is no one at home?'

Madame Beauregard looked at Emma, and then a slow smile spread over her face. 'No, Groumand, send him in.'

'Here, madam. But . . .'

'I said, send him in here!'

'Very good, madam.'

Hope leapt in Emma's bosom. She was facing the door and she stared at it, her whole heart in her eyes.

What happened next was like a nightmare. Dressed in the finest evening dress, jewels winking at his stock and on his fingers, the Comte Saint-Juste strolled into the room. He did not even look at Emma but went straight to Madame Beauregard and bowed over her hand, kissing the air above the back of it.

'Well, Saint-Juste,' said Madame Beauregard, 'you have a cool nerve.'

'I came to present my compliments to the most beautiful woman in London,' said the comte, smiling into her eyes.

So did he once smile on me, thought Emma bleakly as all hope ebbed away.

The comte took a chair and placed it so that he was facing Madame Beauregard, their knees almost touching. Outside, unaware of this macabre scene, London nightlife went on. There was the rumble of carriages as they came and went in Manchester Square, the chatter of voices, the call of the watch, and the shrill voices of the linkboys, their lights bobbing like fireflies past the windows.

'Tell me how you arranged it all, my beloved adversary,' said the comte. 'And why are you still here? You must trust me to keep my mouth shut.'

'I thought our prize here would do that effectively,' said Madame Beauregard, flicking a contemptuous glance at the bound and gagged Emma.

'Oh, no, it is my own skin I am thinking of,' said the comte. 'I am sure you have already made plans to get rid of me. I put it to you thus, my silence for my life and you can do what you will with Lady Wright. She has become a bore.'

'Now I understand you!' laughed Madame Beauregard. 'You are in fact what I thought you always were – a heartless dilettante.'

'You have been very clever,' said the comte, taking her hand and caressing it. 'How did you entrap such a one as Sir Benjamin?'

'T'was easy. He wanted money, that was all, and did not care how he got it. He signed his own death warrant. The fool tried to blackmail me.'

'And so you sent Fletcher to kill him?'

'No, I wished the satisfaction of doing it myself. He had given me keys to the back door of his home and his study. I sent Fletcher to the ball to fetch something of the wife's that might incriminate her. She was so enamoured of you that she dropped her fan and never noticed it. A neat domestic murder, you see. He brought back the fan, I dressed in men's clothes to scale that filthy wall from the mews with ease, and the rest was simple. You should have seen the old fool's face.'

'But it took strength to lift the drugged secretary up on that hook,' said the comte.

'I left that affair to my husband and Fletcher. We will probably spare your life, milor, if you prove you are safe.'

'And how shall I do that, my sweeting?'

'Strangle Lady Wright. I do not want her shot. The watch might become too inquisitive.'

Faint with terror and misery, Emma heard the comte laugh. 'Kiss me first,' she heard him say, 'to give me strength.'

Madame Beauregard rose to her feet and held out her arms. He rose as well. He put one arm around her waist and smiled down at her. Then with his other hand he brought a little green bottle out of his pocket and held it up. 'Perfume from Paris for you, my love,' he said.

He released her for a moment and unscrewed the top. 'Would you like to smell it, *ma chèrie*?' he asked.

'What an odd man you are. I have scent a-plenty.'

'But not like this one,' he said, his arm going around her again and holding her close while with one hand he held up the bottle to the light. 'This one contains acid . . . acid to burn off that pretty face of yours. No! Do not scream. By the time any of your servants arrived, you would have no face left.'

She swore at him furiously in French while her eyes, dilated with terror, never left the bottle he held above her.

'You are so low,' said the comte, 'so base that your mistake was to consider me as low and base as you. Now you will release Lady Wright. Remember, you may turn your face away, you may try to escape, but I am quick and I will succeed in emptying this vial over you before help can reach you. Had I tried to shoot you, you would have let me, for you are a fanatic. You would have died knowing the shot would have alerted your servants and they would have killed myself and Lady Wright. But your vanity is great and you could not bear to have your face ruined, even in death. Odd, is it not? Now release Lady Wright.'

He kept one arm around her waist and urged her forward to the chair on which Emma sat. Emma looked at him with dazed hope, hardly able to believe her ears. 'The knots are too tight, you fool,' hissed Madame Beauregard. 'Then take that knife from the table over there and use it, but remember, one slip of the knife and you are ruined,' the comte said.

Emma sat very still, fearing at any moment to feel the knife being driven into her ribs. One by one the bonds fell away, and Emma herself untied the gag from her mouth.

'Now, madam,' said the comte, 'you will walk to the street door and open it. Tell the servants, should any be around, not to interfere.'

Madame Beauregard looked at him, her face distorted with fear and rage. She slowly walked to the door, the comte supporting her like a lover but holding the green bottle ready.

The hall was empty. Emma walked slowly to the door.

'Open it quickly,' said the comte. 'You will find Jolly outside with the carriage. Go straight away.'

'But you . . .' whispered Emma.

'I have work to do. Go!'

Emma unlocked and unbolted the door. She swayed for a moment on the step, her figure illuminated for a moment by the light over the door, and then she was gone. The comte could hear Jolly's glad cry of welcome.

'Now,' he said to Madame Beauregard, 'back inside.'

'You have what you want,' she said harshly.

'Not all. Where is Sir Benjamin's book?'

'We burnt it.'

'No, you fools felt too secure. Your arrogance had made you make many stupid mistakes. So far luck has been on your side, but that luck has run out.' His eyes raked round the room, and then he began to laugh. 'Why, there it is, for all the world to see!'

He snatched the book from a console table and put it in his pocket. He backed toward the door, while she stood, half crouched, staring at him with eyes full of venom.

'Oh, *ma chèrie*,' he said lightly, 'there is one thing more . . .' He suddenly hurled the contents of the bottle full in her face. Madame Beauregard gave a scream like a mortally wounded animal and fell on the floor, clutching her face while the comte ran out into the street, shouting for the constable, shouting for the watch, at the top of his voice.

Madame Beauregard's husband and Lord Fletcher drew quickly back into the shadows of the square. 'The jig's up,' said Lord Fletcher. 'We must escape alone. Come, man, look at the men and torches. The whole army's descending on the house.'

Madame Beauregard was still lying on the floor where the comte had last seen her when he entered with the militia, the watch and the constable.

She was screaming and moaning and clutching at her face.

'Has she run mad?' asked the colonel of the militia.

'Mad with fear,' said the comte. 'I thought she deserved to suffer for all the misery she has caused.' He seized a mirror and knelt down by Madame Beauregard. 'Hold her hands away from her face,' he ordered.

'Look at yourself,' said the comte. 'Take a look.'

Two men held her arms while another forced her to look in the mirror. She stared at her reflection. Her face, apart from a redness at the eyes, was the same as ever.

'Mustard water,' said the comte cheerfully. 'Not acid. You may take her away.' As he left, he heard her begin to scream again, but this time with rage.

It was late at night when the comte finally made his way to Curzon Street. Jolly was sitting in the hall with a shotgun across his knees, fast asleep, and did not even wake when Tamworthy let the comte in.

'A fine guard you make,' said the comte, shaking his friend awake. 'Where is Lady Wright?'

'Gone to bed,' said Jolly, and then let out a cavernous yawn.

The comte felt disappointed. He had rescued Emma and she should have been there to throw herself into his arms.

'Well, I suppose I had better join you on guard, but we may retire upstairs. There are two members of the militia outside the doors. Madame Beauregard has been taken, but there is no sign of her villainous husband or Fletcher. Do you know Fletcher was seen at the club earlier this evening, as bold as brass? They must have been so sure of their luck holding. I think they were all under Madame Beauregard's sway, and I think that lady is quite mad.'

The pair walked up the stairs together to Emma's drawing room. 'Think, *mon ami*,' said the comte, sinking into an armchair, 'of their incredible stupidity. All they had to do was to take Lady Wright somewhere out of town where we could not find her. Or why not kill her outright and then me? What a night I have had! There is one thing that still puzzles me. Lady Wright was on her way to visit Mrs Carruthers when she was abducted. After the arrest of Madame Beauregard and her servants, we went straight to the Carrutherses' home and interrogated Carruthers himself. Oh, he was very smooth. He had sent no carriage for Lady Wright. He had assumed she had changed her mind. Was it not, he was asked, a coincidence that he had told her the time to come was exactly the hour when it suited Fletcher? For, as you know, the authorities were quick to interrogate the servants here and find that little housemaid had been helping Fletcher, although she thought she was helping a lover. Carruthers gave that easy laugh of his and said he had gossiped the night before to Fletcher of how he had planned to please his wife by inviting Lady Wright. All very simple. But that pretty wife of his looked afraid and miserable. Of course they believed him. Who does not believe a drunk and a gambler? It is only the worthy sober people who are held in suspicion. Carruthers, said the magistrate indulgently, is no end of a good fellow. Pah!'

'So what do we do with Lady Wright while these villains are still at large?' asked Jolly.

'I had better marry her, and then she will have constant protection.'

'Not a sound basis for marriage.'

'There are other factors,' said the comte. 'I am so very tired. Go to bed, Jolly, and I will awaken you in two hours' time and we will change guard. Come, I will show you to the spare bedchamber. The servants have drunk so much consoling brandy, they are probably all asleep by now.'

After Jolly had retired, the comte turned the facts about the traitors over in his mind. In that precious book had been other names, names of men and women who were already being arrested. But money, it seemed, could buy anything in this age of gambling and ruin. He would have to tell Emma not to have anything further to do with the Carrutherses. He was sure Carruthers himself had accepted a large bribe. The traitors seemed to have money to burn. Money could buy conscience, wives, children – his eyelids began to droop – comforts in prison, special treatment, even the loyalty of the guards.

All of a sudden he was wide awake. Perhaps even now Beauregard had found some way to bribe his wife's release from prison. Without their Lady Macbeth, he felt sure Fletcher and Beauregard would be relatively harmless. But with her . . .

He ran to Jolly's room, roused his large friend, and explained his fears.

'Should have taken her to the Tower,' grumbled Jolly. 'Where is she?'

'Newgate.'

'My dear fellow, she is probably chained to the floor!'

'But chains can be removed. I must go.'

'Oh, very well,' grumbled Jolly, climbing down from the bed. 'I will stand guard while you are gone.'

The comte ran from the house to the mews, where his carriage and horses were stabled, rousing his grooms and his grumbling tiger, who protested loudly at the very idea of a drive to Newgate in the middle of the night.

With his swearing tiger clinging on the back, he hurtled toward the City, down Fleet Street, past the silent taverns, across the sluggish, smelly Fleet River, up Ludgate Hill, and under the shadow of St Paul's.

The prison governor was extremely cross. The

hour was four in the morning, and he did not like to be roused by what he privately damned as an excitable Frenchman, demanding to make sure that Madame Beauregard was still locked up.

'My lord,' snapped the governor, struggling with all the disadvantages of trying to be haughty in a red Kilmarnock nightcap and flannel nightgown. 'You should be ashamed of yourself. No one has escaped from Newgate since the days of Jack Shepard. The Frenchwoman is fettered and chained, and no one but the wardresses are allowed near her.'

'Sir, I beg of you,' said the comte, 'please ascertain that she is still secure in this prison.'

'Oh, very well,' grumbled the governor. He rang the bell and ordered his servant to go to the prison and ask the turnkeys to check that Madame Beauregard was still imprisoned.

'You must understand,' said the governor, waxing pompous while they waited, 'that this is not France. We order things better in this country. You appear to suggest that one of my fellows would take a bribe. Ridiculous. Why, if that were the case, half the cells would be empty. I remember the time . . .'

His voice droned on.

The comte heard the commotion before the governor did, and his heart sank.

He held up a hand for silence, and the governor threw him an offended look, which, as he, too, heard the growing noise outside, changed to one of alarm.

His servant burst into the room, his eyes starting from his head.

'She's gone!' he shouted. 'The Frenchie's gone. Her guards were lying outside her cell, drugged!'

Guards crowded in behind the servant.

The governor drew himself to his feet and pointed at the comte. 'Arrest this man,' he commanded. 'I know now why you came here, my lord. It was to keep me occupied while your collaborators released the traitor!'

'My dear governor,' said the comte, striving for calm. 'Only think! Had I not called, you would have been asleep. On what grounds do you accuse me?'

The governor said contemptuously, 'You're French, ain't you?' And as far as everyone but the comte was concerned, that seemed to clinch the matter.

EIGHT

Matilda, Duchess of Hadshire, had defied her husband by calling on Emma the day following Emma's escape, only to be told by a solemn Tamworthy that his lady had retired to a place of safety in the country and had left strict instructions not to tell anyone at all where she had gone.

And so Matilda returned home, wondering about Emma's welfare but glad to be informed when she entered the house that the duke had left for the day with some sporting friends.

She had just removed her bonnet and gloves when a footman came to tell her that Mrs Carruthers had called and was waiting in the saloon.

Matilda went quickly downstairs to find a pale and distraught Annabelle.

'What is it, my dear?' asked Matilda anxiously. 'You look dreadful.'

‘I think my husband is a traitor to his country, and I don’t know what to do,’ said Annabelle, and burst into tears.

‘Shhh, now,’ said Matilda, sitting down beside her on the sofa. ‘Compose yourself and tell me about it. There must be something I can do.’

Annabelle continued to cry. Matilda handed her a dry handkerchief and waited patiently.

At last, in a halting voice, Annabelle told her of the abduction of Emma and how her husband had suddenly come into a very large amount of money.

‘But was he questioned?’ exclaimed Matilda. ‘What did he say?’

‘He said nothing of the money. He merely said he had unfortunately told Fletcher the night before that he had invited Emma to stay with us. Everyone believed him, for he is accounted no end of a good fellow. But I . . . I do not.’

‘I know he is feckless,’ said Matilda. ‘But treason!’

‘But why does he look so guilty when I question him?’

‘Where does he say he got the money from?’

‘He said he had a lucky win at cards, but I cannot believe it. I once heard that when he wins a great deal at cards, he simply stays at the table until he has gambled it all away again.’

Matilda drew a deep breath. ‘Let me have the whole story over again, and slowly this time.’

Annabelle dutifully repeated as much as she knew, how she had been awake early preparing for Emma’s arrival and by ten o’clock had wanted to send the page to find out what had happened to Emma, but her husband had said he had already done so and Emma was not at home.

'If he is guilty of having aided Lord Fletcher,' said Matilda, 'perhaps he merely thought he was helping in a romantic plot. Fletcher would not risk telling Carruthers the real reason for the abduction.'

'Perhaps you have the right of it,' said Annabelle, cheering visibly. 'My husband is weak and . . . and . . . often thoughtless, but I am sure he would do nothing to betray his country.'

Matilda continued to enlarge on the theme of Annabelle's husband's innocence, and at last Annabelle left feeling and looking considerably better. When she had gone, Matilda walked to the mirror and stared at her reflection in the glass. 'You didn't believe a word of what you said,' she told her reflection severely. 'But what would happen to my poor Annabelle should she denounce her husband as a traitor? No one would believe *her* innocence. Perhaps she would be tried along with him if proof could be found. And how would she live? She has no money of her own and he has none to leave her; and *my* husband would certainly not let me help her. I shall keep a sharp eye on Carruthers in the future, and if I can find a way of ruining him without ruining Annabelle at the same time, I will do it!'

After the rest of the night and a whole day in prison, the comte was finally released, thanks to the intervention of his friends, led by Jolly.

'The hour is late,' said the comte to Jolly, 'but I must see Lady Wright.'

'Can't see her tonight!' said Jolly cheerfully. 'She's in the country.'

'Where? At her home? That is the first place they will look if they want revenge.'

'No, I sent her to m'mother. Great sport, m'mother. Lady Wright will have no end of a time.'

The comte felt sad and irritable. He had made up his mind to marry Emma. He felt sure had he struck while the iron was hot – that is, right after his rescue of her, then she would have accepted him. But he feared that Emma, with all her bad experience of marriage, would now not welcome his proposal. Jolly's mother lived in Surrey, a day's drive from London. But the comte was to be questioned at length by several gentlemen at the War Office and had been told to remain in London. They were eager to learn all he could tell them about the traitors. He groaned inwardly. It might be several days before he could see Emma again, several days in which that lady had time to forget his existence. He had not met Jolly's mother and did not like to hear her described as a 'great sport'. That conjured up visions of endless entertaining with Emma being courted by every available man in the county.

Mrs Simpson, Jolly's mother, adjusted her muslin cap and said sharply, 'Continue reading, Lady Wright.'

Emma stifled a sigh and picked up the book that

she had let drop to her lap. '"Count Florimund seized Angela's fainting body in his strong arms and rained kisses down on her pallid face."' While Emma continued to read, only half taking in the words of the novel, she turned over in her mind ways to escape – politely – from Mrs Simpson.

She had expected Jolly's mother to be someone like her son, bluff and hearty and easy-going. But Mrs Simpson had turned out to be a querulous lady, very small and slight, with a withered face covered with strong grey hairs, making her look like some bad-tempered animal aroused from winter hibernation. Her hands were small and fat and red, and encased in string mittens like small joints of meat prepared by the butcher for the oven. Her small feet were fat also and jammed into shoes much too small for them. Her body, in contrast, was thin and smelled strongly of camphor, violet scent and various other nasty odours caused by a reluctance to wash. Her gowns were of the finest, but covered with food stains and snuff stains and wine stains.

She lived in a large house on the top of a knoll, surrounded by lawns on which dejected-looking sheep tore at the short grass. The weather was bad, and sheets of rain lashed the long windows of the drawing room. Rain gurgled in the gutters and dripped down the chimney onto the empty hearth. The house was cold and damp.

Mrs Simpson appeared to regard Emma as an unpaid companion and was constantly ordering her to read or to fetch silks from the work basket or go for walks across the dismal lawns, holding an umbrella with great iron shafts.

Contrary to the comte's expectations, Emma, cold and miserable and bored, thought of him constantly. The passionate scenes in the novels that Mrs Simpson loved only made Emma's body ache with longing. But she was not afraid. From a day-old newspaper she had learned of Madame Beauregard's escape, but felt that even such a formidable enemy would never trace her to this dismal house, where nobody called except the vicar on Sunday evening after evensong.

Mrs Simpson evinced no curiosity about the traitors or their murderous activities. The carrier delivered to her door large supplies of all the latest novels. Mrs Simpson preferred illustrated novels, and when Emma came to a picture she would creep to her feet and lean over Emma's shoulder, studying the illustration, her mouth a little open, and breathing heavily through her nose.

Like most English people, Mrs Simpson detested the French and credited that nationality with all sorts of horrible practices. She told Emma quite solemnly that it was well known that Napoleon ate newly born babies, well-roasted, for his breakfast.

Her servants were old and frail, and Emma could only be glad of her conviction that the Beauregards would never find her because there would certainly be no one to defend her. Giles, the footman, was old and toothless. While Emma was reading, he entered with an armful of logs and slowly subsided on the carpet and lay there panting. Emma made a move to help him, but Mrs Simpson snapped, 'Pay no attention. Giles is like a spoilt child. He will rouse himself eventually.'

Emma continued to read nervously while the footman wheezed creakily to his feet and carried the spilled logs one by one to the log basket by the fire, although why he should even bother to go to the effort of filling the basket when no fires were ever lit seemed a waste of time to Emma.

Then there was the butler, Jensen, a tortoise of a man, never quite drunk and never quite sober. He was *very* old, and wore a wig of spun glass to conceal his baldness and false wooden teeth, of which he was inordinately proud. The housekeeper, Mrs Grant, was also old, and had the knack of apparently being able to fall asleep standing up, like a horse. There were two chambermaids, a parlour maid, three housemaids and a cook. Emma was sure there was not one of them under the age of fifty. They did not talk. She doubted whether they even conversed when they were in the servants' hall. At night, when Mrs Simpson retired to bed at nine o'clock, the house settled down into black silence, except for the noise of the clocks. There were a great many clocks – grandfather clocks, ornamental clocks, clocks housed in black marble temples, clocks supported by frivolous shepherds and shepherdesses – all set at different times and all ticking and tocking and chiming out the hours.

Mrs Simpson did not read the newspapers, but

the butler did, and one morning Emma waylaid him and asked him if she might have a look at a paper.

As usual, Jensen did not reply, but he shuffled off and returned an hour later carrying a copy of the *Morning Post*. Emma read it quickly, eager to get through as much of it as possible before Mrs Simpson came downstairs and the day's reading of novels began.

There was still a long story about the hunt for the traitors. They were believed to have escaped to France. Emma turned to the social column, and the comte's name seemed to leap up at her out of the page. 'At Lady Harvey's ball,' she read, 'the Comte Saint-Juste delighted the company with a clever display of card tricks.'

A leaden feeling stole over her. She forgot the comte's bravery; she remembered only how frivolous he was. Here she was, immured in this dreadful house, while he made a fool of himself at the Harveys' ball.

Her lips set in a firm line. Enough was enough! She looked out the window. The sun was actually shining, turning the raindrops clinging to the ivy at the window into diamonds.

She ran lightly upstairs and changed into a walking dress and a serviceable pair of half boots. She knew there was a town some two miles away beyond the lodge gates of the Simpson estate. She would walk there and order a post-chaise to take her back to London on the morrow. She bitterly regretted having allowed Jolly to talk her into leaving her carriage behind, not to mention the faithful Austin.

Jolly distrusted all Emma's servants because of the treachery of the housemaid.

Emma's spirits began to lift as she walked down the long drive between the sodden lawns. The sky above was pale blue, and a gentle breeze ruffled the pools of rainwater on the grass.

Feeling much better than she had done in a long time, she walked out of the estate and along a country road where high hedges bordered either side, turning the road into a long green tunnel.

She had been at Jolly's mother's for only a little over a week, but the sight of the market town of Tadminster was a delight. To see relatively young people moving about the streets was a joy. The air was full of the chatter of voices. She asked directions to the livery stables, made her way there, and ordered the post-chaise and paid in advance. She was turning around, ready to return, when she felt she could not bear to leave all this light and colour and noise behind to become immured once more in that gloomy, cold drawing room with Mrs Simpson. Emma realized she was hungry. There was a prosperous-looking posting house in the town. She opened the door, went into the coffee room, and ordered a pot of coffee and hot rolls and jam, and feeling pleasurably guilty, like a child playing truant from school, she demolished the lot.

Madame Beauregard was sitting in a closed carriage at a corner of the town square with Lord Fletcher. Their appearances were greatly altered. Madame Beauregard had dyed her hair black and

Lord Fletcher wore plain clothes and had stuck a fine false pair of military side whiskers on his face.

'Let's hope Beauregard finds word of her,' said Fletcher peevishly. 'This is madness with the whole of England looking for us. Why did we not just escape to the coast when we had the chance?'

'They must be shown that we, Napoleon's still-loyal followers, are a force to be reckoned with,' said Madame Beauregard. 'I will never forgive Saint-Juste. And what better way to punish him than to destroy his lady love.'

The carriage door opened and Beauregard slipped inside. 'She is sitting in the coffee room of that inn,' he said. 'I went there to see if I could find out if anyone knew anything about the Simpson house and who was staying there. Before I went into the inn, I looked in at the coffee room window and there she was!'

Madame Beauregard's eyes shone. 'Good!' She drew up the carriage blind and looked out. 'We will watch and see when she leaves. There might be some way we can waylay her on the way back.'

She waited impatiently and then at last saw Emma's slim figure leaving the inn.

Emma was just crossing the square, very near the carriage that held the Beauregards and Lord Fletcher, when she heard a female voice calling, 'Lady Wright?'

She turned round. An open carriage carrying three young ladies was standing in the square, and the one who had called to her was getting down. She was a bouncing girl with red ringlets and a saucy hat. She came up to Emma. 'It is Lady Wright, is it not?' she asked eagerly.

Emma smiled in assent and curtsied. 'I am Miss Johnson,' said the girl, holding out her hand, 'and these giggling reprobates in the carriage are my sisters. The vicar told us of your arrival, and we have been dying to hear all about your adventures, but it is well known that Mrs Simpson don't receive anyone. Are you walking back? May we take you up?'

'Thank you, Miss Johnson,' said Emma. 'I would enjoy your company. It seems a long time since I have talked to anyone under the age of fifty. How did you recognize me?'

'Oh,' giggled Miss Johnson. 'Our good vicar's description was most detailed.'

Emma climbed into the carriage with the girls and answered their eager questions as best she could on the road home.

'You had better drop me at the lodge,' said Emma finally. 'I shall be in trouble enough with Mrs Simpson when she finds I am leaving.'

Emma climbed down and then reached up to shake hands in farewell with the Johnson girls. She then turned her head as if aware of being watched. There was a closed carriage waiting at the bend of the road. The driver on the box had a muffler around the lower half of his face and a hat pulled down over his eyes. Emma felt a sudden shiver of dread and then mentally shook herself. The carriage was waiting for the Johnson girls to move on because the road was too narrow to allow any carriage to pass them.

She walked past the lodge gates and up the long drive, turning after a little while and looking back. But the high hedge in the road screened any carriage from view.

Mrs Simpson did not receive the news of Emma's going at all well and spoke for almost the first time of the real reason for Emma's visit. 'You are very silly, Lady Wright,' grumbled Mrs Simpson. 'I had a letter from my son to say that he and that Frenchman will be calling any day now.'

'Why did you not tell me?' cried Emma. 'Did they say exactly when they would arrive?'

'No, and you will take my advice and have nothing to do with a Frenchman. Your late husband was a good, solid Englishman.'

'My late husband, madam, was a traitor.'

'Oh, so he was and more fool him. Never mind. You are young and flighty and will change your mind on the morrow.'

But Emma was determined to go. If the comte came and missed her, then it was his own fault. He might at least have written to her.

That afternoon she wearily read to Mrs Simpson and, as if to match her mood, the day grew dark outside and the rain began to fall.

Before supper that evening, Emma, with the creaking help of an elderly chambermaid, packed her trunks. Mrs Simpson considered the employment of lady's maids frivolous.

Now that she was ready to leave in the morning, Emma began to feel almost affectionate toward her odd hostess and volunteered to read to her after supper for a little.

Mrs Simpson had a new novel called *Lord Randolph's Revenge, or, How Purity and Simplicity Can Melt a Heart of Stone.* It was well illustrated with lurid steel engravings.

Emma was well launched on the first chapter when there came a furious knocking at the door. She sprang to her feet, pink colour staining her pale cheeks. He had come! All her doubts and worries about the comte fled. She took a half step to the door, but Mrs Simpson snapped, 'Sit down, girl. I don't have callers.'

'But your son . . . ?'

'My son arrives tomorrow with that Frenchie.'

'You should have told me earlier! If you had told me when you received the letter, then I would have waited for them. You only said they *might* arrive any day.'

'I did it for your own good. I have taken a liking to you and have no wish to see you in the toils of a Frog. What is it, Jensen?'

'There are three persons to see you, madam.'

The butler stood in the shadowy doorway. He appeared to be trembling, but, then, he always shook a little.

'What has come over you, Jensen? I don't see people, and I definitely don't see persons. Send them away.'

'I would, madam, but one of the persons has a gun at my back.'

The butler walked slowly into the room. Emma

rose to her feet again and faced the door. Behind Jensen walked the Beauregards and Lord Fletcher. Lord Fletcher had the gun. The three had been delighted to hear stories in the town of Mrs Simpson's elderly retinue of servants.

Madame Beauregard raised the heavy veil she wore over her face and stared at Emma, her eyes glittering with venom.

'I would like to see you die slowly, Emma Wright,' she said, 'but we will make it quick.'

Giles, the footman, shuffled into the room with a tea tray which he placed on the table in front of Mrs Simpson.

'Get out of the way, you old fool,' Lord Fletcher snapped. 'Lady Wright, stand aside or we will kill them as well as you.'

Giles straightened up and stared in amazement at the gun in Lord Fletcher's hand. There was a shuffling in the doorway and the rest of the old household servants, attracted by the commotion, came to see what was the matter.

'Oh, no,' said the old footman, slowly shaking his head. 'We can't have guns here, sir.'

Lord Fletcher raised his pistol. 'Stand back!' he shouted, but the footman continued to advance on him, shaking his hoary locks and champing his toothless gums.

'Shoot him and let's get on with it,' commanded Madame Beauregard.

Lord Fletcher pulled the trigger and fired, but the ball went whizzing harmlessly over the footman's head, for Giles had sunk to his knees in front of Lord Fletcher and had grasped him round the knees. 'No, no,' he mumbled. 'Can't have guns.'

Beauregard ran forward and tried to pull the old footman away, and Lord Fletcher went toppling to the floor.

Mrs Simpson, with amazing speed, jumped on his hand that held the pistol and then snatched it up. 'Get them!' she screamed, dancing from foot to foot. 'Get the traitors!'

The butler flung himself on top of Beauregard and Lord Fletcher and began kicking and punching and gouging while Madame Beauregard backed to the window as what seemed to her a whole army of gibbering and mouthing ancient females advanced on her.

Mrs Simpson seemed beside herself with glee. She grabbed the poker and began cracking it down on the writhing figures on the floor. Emma seized her work scissors and cut the bell rope, and as a final couple of cracks rendered both Fletcher and Beauregard senseless, she knelt down and began to tie their hands behind their backs.

Madame Beauregard was screaming like an animal. 'I'll hit her as well,' cried Mrs Simpson, rushing forward with the poker.

But Madame Beauregard had suddenly fallen silent. As the maidservants who had pummelled her to the floor hoisted her to her feet, she stood swaying in their grasp, her eyes empty, a thin line of spittle running down her chin.

'She has lost her reason,' whispered Emma, and sat down on a chair, suddenly weak with shock.

'I trounced 'em,' yelled the indomitable Mrs Simpson. 'Just like Count Florimund did the Turk. Tie up that mad woman as well and then one of you go and get the militia. Giles, you may take my best horse.'

The old footman's eyes gleamed. 'I shall ride like the wind,' he croaked, leaving Emma, despite her shock and fear and distress, to register that the servants probably read all the romances that their mistress had finished with.

'Hear ye! Hear ye! Hear ye!' called the town crier in the centre square of Tadminster.

Jolly reined in his horse and called to the comte, who was looking impatiently over his shoulder to see what was delaying his friend. 'Wait a bit. Let's hear the news.'

The comte stopped and waited while Jolly's horse minced up alongside his own.

'Why do we wait?' demanded the comte. 'It will be the usual rural news.'

'Shhh!' admonished Jolly.

'Hear ye,' said the crier. 'Last evening in the parish of St George, Mrs Simpson, relict of the late Mr Geoffrey Simpson, did trounce and capture three French traitors who sought to kill Lady Wright, relict of the late Sir Benjamin Wright, Member of Parliament. Said traitors were taken to the round-house and this day will be conveyed to the Tower to meet the fate of all traitors against this glorious realm. God save the King!'

'Don't that beat all?' exclaimed Jolly. 'The old Trojan.'

'Come on, man,' said the comte. 'Lady Wright may have been hurt in some way.'

When they reached Mrs Simpson's house, they found the door open and a great noise coming from the drawing room. They made their way there.

The servants and Emma and various officials formed an audience while Mrs Simpson stood on a chair, brandishing a poker and re-enacting her victory.

Emma turned and saw the comte. She blushed a vivid colour and, suddenly shy, looked at the floor.

While Mrs Simpson continued her tale, the comte found himself cursing inwardly. What a feeble fellow her heroism was making him look! He had left Emma in danger, and instead of being able to rescue her himself, that rescue had been performed by Jolly's horrible mother and a band of creaking servants, most of them women.

At last Mrs Simpson finished to loud applause. The comte took Emma aside and said, 'Come out to the gardens with me. There is much I have to say to you.'

Emma was back in mourning, he noticed. The blackness of her gown accentuated her pallor. There were blue shadows under her eyes and slight hollows in her cheeks.

She walked out of the house with him. It was a

glorious morning, glittering and sparkling with a busy wind pushing huge white clouds like galleons across a cerulean sky.

'I am desperately sorry I was not here to protect you,' said the comte.

Emma gave a fleeting glance at him. He looked as debonair as ever. His top boots were burnished to a high shine, and despite his journey there was not even one speck of mud on his breeches or on his deep-blue coat or his snowy linen.

Some imp urged her to say, 'It must have been much more entertaining in the drawing rooms of London. I read of your card tricks.'

'And disapproved? But I had to make myself available during the day for several boring old gentlemen who spent their days asking me endless and tedious questions as if by boring me to death they could elicit from my last gasp the names of yet more spies.'

Emma would have thought it more seemly if he had spent his evenings in solitary splendour, thinking of her, but could hardly say so.

'But despite your fright, you were well entertained by Jolly's mother, *hein*? She is, as he says, a great sport.'

'I am deeply indebted to her and her servants,' said Emma, 'but I would not describe her as a great sport. She treated me as an unpaid companion, and I had to spend my days reading dreadful romances to her.'

'My poor love.'

Emma looked at him, startled.

'Lady Wright . . . Emma . . . what I really want to say to you . . . to ask you, is . . . oh, what is it?'

He had just been on the point of taking Emma's hands in his own when a silver tray with two brimming champagne glasses on it was thrust between them.

'Champagne, my lord, my lady,' cackled Giles. 'A celebration.'

'Thank you,' said the comte bleakly.

'Giles was so very brave,' said Emma. 'It was he who attacked Lord Fletcher.'

'Yes, yes,' said the comte. 'You are indeed a brave man.'

'I says to him, I says,' mumbled Giles, 'we'll have no guns here. That's what I said. He looked at me and his eyes were red like those of a fiend from hell. But that did not stop me. I knew my duty. I grasped him round the knees like this . . .' The footman creaked down onto the grass and laid the tray tenderly on the lawn and then put his arms around the comte's boots.

'Thank you,' said the comte, trying to extricate himself. 'That will be all. We shall call you later and you may tell us the full account of your heroism.'

'He fell to the floor,' droned Giles as if the comte has not spoken, 'and he smelled of the pit. I am wrestling with the devil, I thought.'

The comte leaned down and put his hands under the footman's armpits and raised him by force to his feet. 'I hear them calling for you indoors,' he said.

'We must not be selfish and keep you here when so many wish to hear your story.'

Giles shambled off after picking up the tray.

'It seems very early in the day to be drinking champagne or . . . or anything,' said Emma nervously.

'Oh, *damme* the champagne,' said the comte, taking her glass from her and throwing it across the lawn and hurling his own after it. 'Emma, for God's sake, will you marry me?'

Emma experienced a great rush of gladness followed by one of fear. She was no longer an innocent virgin. What if this handsome French count should turn out to be a monster in the bedchamber like her husband? All the yearnings she had experienced for him while he had been absent fled to be replaced by doubt and uncertainty.

She hung her head. 'I do n-not know,' she stammered. 'Please give me time.'

'No,' he said. 'If I give you time, you will worry and fret yourself into believing me a man such as your husband. Look at me, Emma!'

She looked up into his eyes, at the love and warmth and tenderness there, and felt her legs turn to jelly. He put his hands lightly on her shoulders and drew her to him. When his lips met hers, it was gently and warmly, not fiercely or passionately. There was nothing to fear. It was like coming home.

There was a commotion from the house, the sound of the officials taking their leave. The couple broke apart.

Mrs Simpson ambled out onto the lawn and moved toward Emma. 'I have decided, my dear, and so I told Peter, that you must remain here with me to recuperate from your adventures.'

'I am afraid I cannot,' said Emma firmly. 'I have a house in London I wish to redecorate and much to see to.'

'Lady Wright will be perfectly safe with Jolly and me,' put in the comte.

'Humph!' said Mrs Simpson, who obviously still did not approve of the comte. 'We would never have become involved in all this French business had it not been for you.'

'Now, that is not fair,' said Emma sharply. 'The Comte Saint-Juste was eager to clear my name, which is why he interested himself in my husband's murder in the first place.'

Under her grey whiskers, Mrs Simpson's face fell. Emma saw the loneliness in the old lady's eyes and said impulsively, 'Return with me, Mrs Simpson, as my guest. You may stay as long as you please.'

She caught a cynical glance from the comte and coloured. Her generous impulse, she knew all at once, appeared to him as simply a ruse to avoid answering his proposal, and, in a way, she was suddenly sure he was in part correct.

How could she explain to this very worldly and sophisticated French count her fear of the intimacies of the bedchamber?

He and Jolly elected to stay the night at Mrs Simpson's and make their journey on the following day. The comte appeared to have withdrawn behind a barrier of frivolity. He entertained Emma, Jolly and his mother with all the London gossip, but Emma felt he had cut himself off from her and never guessed for one moment how badly his pride had been wounded.

The comte had never proposed marriage to any woman before, and was angry that she did not appear to want him; and, yet, the more distant he became the more wretched Emma felt and she longed to see his customary affection for her back in his eyes.

When they finally reached London, he left Emma and Mrs Simpson at Curzon Street with punctilious politeness. He did not say he would call on her or refer to his proposal of marriage, and Emma retired to her bedchamber and to the administrations of Austin, feeling close to tears.

It was only on the following day that Emma realized the full impact of what her generous offer of hospitality was to mean. Mrs Simpson, surrounded by London bookshops and all the latest novels, was ready to embark on an orgy of reading, except the reading was to be done by Emma.

The house smelled uncomfortably of new paint and new plaster. Outside, the world went about its business and inside Emma read to Mrs Simpson, just as if she were still immured in the country.

Two days passed and still there was no sign of the comte. At last Emma felt she could not bear it any longer and sent a message to Matilda, asking her to meet her at Mrs Trumpington's, and left her maid, Austin, to take over the chore of reading.

Mrs Trumpington was delighted to welcome Emma, who also received a rapturous welcome from Matilda, who was already there and waiting for her. After Emma had recounted her latest adventures and Mrs Trumpington had fallen into her customary afternoon sleep, Matilda leaned forward and said, 'I wonder what is keeping Annabelle.'

'I did not invite her,' said Emma in a low voice. 'You see, it was all most odd, the way Fletcher knew that I was going to the Carrutherses and waylaid me.'

'Annabelle was very worried and distressed by that,' said Matilda. 'But you know, she feels he might be telling the truth in that he said he had told Fletcher about your visit the evening before.'

'But you do not?'

'Well, I do think Annabelle's husband is a wastrel. On the other hand, you cannot think for a moment that Annabelle had a hand in it.'

'Of course not.'

'And with no more money to earn from the traitors, if they did pay him, Carruthers is no longer a threat.'

'Nooo,' said Emma slowly. 'But I do not trust Carruthers, and Annabelle would see that distrust in my face and perhaps might be worried and frightened by it.'

Matilda sighed. 'She is already a worried and frightened woman. But you yourself still look scared,

Emma. I thought you would be so happy now that you are free of threat and free from censure.'

Emma twisted a cambric handkerchief between her fingers. 'It is the Comte Saint-Juste. He has asked me to marry him.'

'And what is the problem? You have no need to marry, and if you do not love him, you are under no obligation to accept his proposal.'

'I long for him,' said Emma, tears starting to her eyes, 'and yet I am frightened of him at the same time. It is the intimacies of marriage, Matilda . . .'

Matilda thought of her own unhappy experience and repressed a shudder.

'Take him!' said Mrs Trumpington, startling them both. 'A fine man like that. Good legs. Keep you amused.'

'I did not reply to his proposal,' said Emma. 'I invited Mrs Simpson to London out of compassion, for I feel she is so very lonely, but I could see the comte thought it was simply a way of not facing up to his proposal. I . . . I have not seen him since.'

'He must be very hurt,' said Matilda. 'You should have said something one way or the other, Emma. If you are this miserable without him, you had better accept him.'

'Yes, I am miserable,' said Emma. 'What shall I do?'

'Get it over with,' said Matilda in her usual forthright way, so much at odds with her delicate appearance. 'Write to him and then invite us all to dance at your wedding!'

NINE

'You are not much fun anymore,' grumbled Jolly. 'All you do is bite a chap's head off.'

'I am bored,' said the comte lightly, 'and so I take it out on you. What shall we do today?'

'Leave London and go to Brighton,' said Jolly promptly. 'There ain't nobody in town worth knowing. Get some sea breezes to blow your megrims away.'

'Perhaps you have the right of it, and yet . . .'

'And yet, Emma Wright is still in London. I went over the other day and she was reading by the yard to m'mother. 'Course with my mother for company, she's well entertained.'

The comte thought privately that Mrs Simpson, brave and redoubtable as she had proved to be, was nonetheless one of the most boring eccentrics he had come across in a long time. His anger with

Emma was in part because she had not taken the trouble to reply to his proposal, and in part because she preferred to read trash all day long to a smelly old woman rather than do anything to seek out his company.

Perhaps it *would* be better to go to Brighton, where the Prince Regent and his retinue were already in residence, and take up his old frivolous life.

His manservant entered with a letter on a tray. 'Delivered by hand, my lord,' he said.

The comte was about to toss it aside, when he was suddenly sure he recognized that handwriting. He cracked open the seal.

'"Dear Comte Saint-Juste,"' he read. '"I wish to accept your proposal of marriage. Yr Humble and Obedient Servant, Emma Wright."'

He felt exactly as if a skyrocket had gone off inside him.

'Won the lottery?' asked Jolly. 'Told you 937 would come up.'

'Better than any lottery,' said the comte dreamily. 'She's going to marry me.'

'Thank goodness for that,' said Jolly. 'You'll find it was my mother who brought her up to the mark. Great old rip, my mother.'

Mrs Simpson was standing by the window of Emma's drawing room, waiting for the delivery of a parcel of new books, when she saw the comte climbing down from his carriage.

'Tcha!' she said over her shoulder to Emma. 'Here's that Frog.'

Emma ran to the glass, patted her curls, and pinched her lips to bring some more colour into them. 'I'll tell that Tamworthy to send him on his way,' said Mrs Simpson.

'Oh, no!' gasped Emma. 'You see, I sent for him.'

'I will never understand why you and my son like the company of that scapegrace,' said Mrs Simpson. 'But there is no call for me to see him. I am going to my room. Let me know when he has gone and, if those books arrive, tell Austin to bring them to me.'

Emma nodded, barely hearing her. She felt very nervous. She could hardly remember what the comte looked like. She had thought about him, transposing his face in her imagination onto the features of every fictional hero in Mrs Simpson's novels.

He strode into the room and looked around him. 'I see the newly plastered walls but no redecoration,' he said. 'How can you bear to live in a gloomy place like this?'

'If you recall,' said Emma tartly, 'I am but returned to town.'

'So you are,' he said with a sudden heart-wrenching smile. 'It seems like years. I waited and waited to hear from you.'

'Sit down, my lord,' said Emma formally. 'We must discuss plans for our wedding.'

'I feel like punishing you by telling you I have changed my mind,' said the comte, 'but, then, that would only punish me. So what do you want, my love? A grand wedding, a quiet wedding, an elopement?'

'I would like to be married from my village. I thought I would see you first and then travel there to tell the happy news to my parents and begin the arrangements.'

'How very efficient. And when is the happy event to take place?'

'I thought . . . I thought next spring.'

'Think again, light of my life. *I* have a special licence in my pocket and *I* would like to get married in a few weeks' time.'

'But that would mean marrying in London! And so soon!' said Emma wretchedly. Now that he was here before her, he was no longer the hero of her dreams, some androgynous Greek god, but a very attractive and masculine man who exuded an aura of sensuality.

He learned forward and said earnestly. 'It is commendable you want to go home. But think of those unnatural parents of yours.'

'You have never met them,' said Emma defensively.

'No, but think on it. You have featured largely in the columns of the newspapers. I would have expected an anxious mama to be at your side, not Jolly's horrible mother.'

Emma gave a startled gurgle of laughter. 'Oh, she *is* so tiresome. She has a constant need to be read to.' A shadow crossed her face. 'But my parents have many concerns to keep them in the country. Perhaps they feel guilty, for it was they who insisted I marry Sir Benjamin.'

The comte leaned back in his chair and studied

her thoughtfully for a few moments. Then he said, 'Go home by all means. Write to me from there and I will come and visit you. You have had a terrible time and must long for the reassurance of your parents' company. But I still insist that their behaviour toward you lacks a great deal of warmth.'

'What shall I do with Mrs Simpson?'

'Give her her marching orders.'

'It will be difficult. She is so very lonely.'

'Then it is time Jolly took over. He admires his mother immensely. He can take her to Brighton.'

The comte rose to his feet and walked over to where Emma was sitting. He bent down and took her hands in his. She looked up into his blue eyes, half shy, half frightened.

'Don't be away from me too long,' he said huskily.

He bent lower.

'Still here?' demanded Mrs Simpson's voice from the doorway.

The comte stifled an oath and straightened up. Emma told Mrs Simpson of her engagement, and that lady looked startled and displeased. The comte waited for Emma to send Mrs Simpson from the room and was very cross indeed when she showed no signs of doing so.

He eventually took his leave without having had the opportunity to snatch even one kiss.

Emma then braced herself to tell Mrs Simpson of the proposed visit to Upper Tipton, but, before she could suggest that Mrs Simpson make preparations to join her son, that lady said, 'Thank you, my dear,' and kissed her warmly. 'I was so lonely and bored before I met you. There is nothing I like more than jaunting about the countryside. I will go and set that lazy maid of yours to packing right away!'

Only a few hours after Emma's arrival in Upper Tipton, it became all too clear to her that her parents thought she had failed them by proposing to marry a Frenchman. They felt, too, that 'poor' Sir Benjamin had been a victim of unscrupulous French people. Everyone knew that nationality was devious and tricky. They were immersed in the small minutiae of village life. Emma's adventures were somehow considered all part of the *foreignness* of the big city and a threat to their ordered and provincial existence.

But it took Emma's mother a full week to voice her real fears. 'Do you remember Jane's Mr Worthing?'

'Oh, yes,' said Emma coldly. 'He cannot have cared for her very much to cry off.'

'But we have been trying to tell you. Of course you do not know, for Jane is visiting the Plumleys in Lower Hardworth. She is engaged again! Mr Worthing is such a fine man. But you see, my love, I do not know how he will take the news of your marriage to a Frenchman.'

'This is ridiculous!' said Emma. 'Mother, the Comte Saint-Juste is a loyal subject of King George. Without his help, I might have found myself accused of my husband's murder.'

'I am sure that cannot be the case,' said Mrs Anstey, looking like a stubborn rabbit. 'Then the village people – well, we must set them a good example. They cannot, naturally, abide the French. Why, only last week at the fair there was this French acrobat and they tarred and feathered him.'

'Oh, the poor man!' cried Emma.

'Nonsense. He was *French*!'

'Mother, what you are trying to say is that you would rather I were married elsewhere?'

'It really would be best for all of us. Besides, you are not of *us* anymore, dear. You have become so Londonized. You would be better there with your grand friends. We do not understand London people. Take that Mrs Simpson. She is upsetting the household with her constant demands to be read to when you are not present.'

'Mrs Simpson and her servants saved my life.'

'Yes, to be sure, and it was monstrous brave of her, but it is upsetting to have to house a lady who goes about cracking people on the head with a poker.'

'I will leave today, Mother. I shall be married in London, and none of you need to attend my wedding if you don't want to.'

Mrs Anstey began to cry. 'We are thinking only of you,' she said between sobs. 'I mean, you would not like to thrust this wedding to a foreigner on our village.'

Emma felt shaken and disgusted. There was really only one thing to do – return to London and let the comte arrange the marriage.

But on the road back, something inside her rebelled. She would not be rushed into a hole-and-corner wedding. She would have a grand society affair and – yes – her dear friends, Annabelle and Matilda, would be her maids of honour.

'I tell you, you ain't going and that's that,' said Mr Carruthers sulkily.

'But why?' wailed Annabelle. 'It's not as if it will cost you any money. Emma is to supply my gown.'

'You are my wife and you will obey me,' roared Mr Carruthers.

'I wish to God I weren't your wife,' said Annabelle. 'I am sure there is something havey-cavey about all this. I think you took money from Fletcher in return for your help in arranging Emma's abduction. Yes, you should be in the Tower along with the rest of them!'

Mr Carruthers jumped to his feet and struck his wife a cruel blow across the face. 'There!' he panted. 'Never speak to me like that again, or it will be the worse for you! You are not going and that is that!'

Over in Grosvenor Square, Matilda, Duchess of Hadshire, was fairing little better.

'It is not convenient,' said the duke icily. 'I detest Saint-Juste.'

'What did he ever do to you?' demanded Matilda, outraged. 'You barely know the man.'

The duke raised his quizzing glass and studied his wife with disfavour. 'Saint-Juste had the temerity to tell me once that my coat, that is, mark you, my claret-coloured coat with the silver buttons, was *badly cut.* So you are not going to that mountebank's wedding, or it will be the worse for you!'

* * *

The comte, in answer to Emma's desperately worded note, found her sitting in her drawing room with her friends' rejection of her wedding invitations lying on her lap.

'What will I do?' said Emma miserably.

'You will leave everything to me,' he said. 'We will be married tomorrow by special licence, by the special licence I have been carrying around this age. That fright, Mrs Simpson, can see you off, and since Jolly is back from Brighton, he can be my bride-man. It is I you are marrying, not some parcel of relatives, not some fair-weather friends. And we are not spending our wedding night in this house. I shall book us the best rooms at a good inn at Richmond on the river. And there is something I must say to you to allay your fears. You may have your own room.'

Emma looked at him, tears of gratitude filling her eyes.

'You think I did not know?' he said softly. 'Of course that monster of a husband of yours has left you with many fears. So we will take things slowly and get to know each other first.'

Emma threw herself into his arms, crying and calling him the best of men.

'There'll be time enough for all that afterward,' said Mrs Simpson, walking in on them. 'I hope you're just leaving, Saint-Juste, for this monstrous exciting novel has just been delivered.'

Emma looked at the books she held in her hands. Six volumes.

As she walked with the comte to the door, she whispered, 'I am not marrying you just to get away from Jolly's mother,' and he whispered back mockingly, 'I will try to believe you.'

And so Emma was married in a small, dark church off the Strand. There had been no time to have a proper wedding gown made, and so she was married in a white ballgown and wearing her finest jewels. The comte almost outshone her in white satin embroidered with gold thread.

She left the church on the arm of her husband, feeling dazed. It had all seemed so quick. The rehearsal in the morning had seemed much longer.

The comte had said, as the service was to be in the afternoon, they would head straight for Richmond and forget about the added ceremony of a wedding breakfast.

Emma turned before she climbed in the carriage and hugged Mrs Simpson. 'I shall miss you,' she lied, and tears gushed to Mrs Simpson's eyes.

'Do not worry, Ma,' said her son, enveloping her in a bear hug and watching the stately progress of the comte's carriage down the street. 'I have an idea.'

The comte seemed content to sit beside Emma and talk lightly about the houses and mansions they passed on their way out of London and tell amusing stories of their inhabitants.

Emma felt she should feel carefree and secure. He had said she would have a separate room at the inn.

But she could not help feeling he might have shown himself more of the lover.

She cast sidelong glances at his handsome face, wondering uneasily if he planned to find intimacy outside marriage as so many members of London society did.

They were alone in a closed carriage, side by side, and now legally wed, but the comte did not appear to want to take the slightest advantage of the situation.

The sun was sinking behind the trees, and there was a nip of frost in the air. *It will be all the same after all*, thought Emma, bewildered. *Our servants, including my dear Austin, are in the carriage behind. We will go to our separate chambers and meet at mealtimes.*

The comte's carriage turned into the courtyard of an inn on the river. A footman opened the door and helped Emma and the comte to alight.

The comte was about to lead Emma into the inn when he saw a sight that stopped him in his tracks. The windows of the coffee room on the ground floor were brightly lit, and there in the bay were the unmistakable figures of Jolly and his mother.

He seized Emma by the arm and swung her around. He picked her up and threw her up onto the box of his carriage – the box that his coachman had just vacated. He called down to the startled servants, who were staring up at them.

'Do not worry. We wish to be private. Tell Mr Simpson to meet all expenses until our return.' And then he urged the team of horses forward until the coach was bowling quickly down the road away from the inn.

'What do you mean, Mr Simpson will pay expenses?' asked Emma.

'Did you not see them?' said the comte savagely. 'Jolly and his mother awaiting us. They must have sprung their horses and passed us on the road.'

'But *why*?' wailed Emma.

'Perhaps, my sweeting, because you gave the old trout the idea you could not live without her.'

'Where are we going?'

'Anywhere where Mrs Simpson is not!'

The moon was shining brightly and the night was by now very cold when he finally drove into the courtyard of a small inn on a by-road.

He called to a boy in the yard to hold the horses' reins and then leapt down and went around the carriage and lifted Emma down from the box.

'It is all my fault,' said Emma miserably. 'I was feeling sorry for Mrs Simpson and said I would miss her.'

'And so she decided she would join us on our wedding night. No matter. Come, my love, and let us see what this landlord can offer.'

The inn was poor and the landlord could offer them only a small bedchamber dominated by a large fourposter. But the linen and blankets were clean and a brisk fire crackled on the hearth.

A man carried in their trunks and bowed his nose almost to the ground when the comte handed him a crown.

'We will change for supper,' said the comte when they were alone. 'We will attract too much attention in all our finery if this miserable place has any other guests.'

He began to strip off his wedding clothes. Emma sat primly on the edge of the bed and stared at the floor.

He had undressed down to his smallclothes when he realized she was still sitting there silently, not making a move.

He came and knelt before her, and Emma averted her eyes from his naked chest.

'My little love,' he said, taking her hands in his. 'I am changing for dinner, not preparing for a rape.'

'Please kiss me,' whispered Emma in a small voice.

He sat beside her on the bed and gathered her into his arms. He removed her bonnet and tossed it on the bed behind them and then began to kiss her gently until the passion in the lips below his own made him murmur something throatily and gather her closer.

At last he freed his mouth and looked down into her dazed face. 'Tell me when to stop,' he murmured.

Emma nodded dumbly, and he fell to kissing her again while his busy hands slid her out of her pelisse and began to loosen the tapes of her gown. At last she lay under him, panting, naked except for the diamonds around her neck.

She put her hands on his shoulders and pushed him a little away. 'I must ask you something . . .'

'Oh, not now, my heart,' groaned the comte.

'I do not know your name,' whispered Emma.

'Is that all? Jules.'

'Oh, Jules, please . . . please . . .'

'Please what?'

'Say you love me.'

'Emma mine, with all my heart and soul and body I love you and will be yours forever. And now let me show you how much . . .'

'Jules,' said Emma after a little while. 'Oh, Jules, please . . .'

'Please what?'

'Please do that again!'

Jolly's eyes strayed from the printed page. He had, he realized, never read to his mother before. He hoped the comte was enjoying himself, for he, Jolly, was most certainly not.

'Pay attention,' snapped Mrs Simpson, 'and go back and read that bit about where the wicked count ravishes the heroine.'

'Yes, Mother,' said Jolly wearily, and fell to reading again.